VOYAGE TO AYAMA

DAWNBREAKER BOOK ONE

K.A. KNIGHT

DEDICATION_

To the copious amounts of wine I drank while writing this, because wine is always the answer.

"Throw your dreams into space like a kite, and you do not know what it will bring back, a new life, a new friend, a new love, a new country."
-Anais Nin

TRANSMISSION LOG 00015
    DATE: 2032
    MISSION: 43, COLONY
    SHIP: DAWNBREAKER
    DESTINATION: AYAMA

>.............. Accepted
> Any news from Ayama? Rumours have gotten
around, there must be a break in the chain of
command. A rebellion naming themselves The
Saviours has started, they claim to know.
Advise on how to proceed?

CHAPTER ONE

A YEAR AGO

OUR HOUSING UNIT is still a mess from my birthday two days ago. I plop my bag down on the table and clear the remaining cake and presents away, and I've just spread my books out on the metal table when the bing sounds from the comms unit. I groan, what now? My mother's voice breaks through my thoughts.

"Indy, you there?" Her velvety voice comes over the speakers as if she is in the room.

With a sigh, I trudge to the comms unit in the kitchen, pressing the talk back button. "Yeah, everything okay?"

"Yes love, how was school?"

I'm betting she's knee deep in some secret experiment right now, she has been for weeks. I barely see her or dad, with the exception being my birthday, and she called it school, really? More like college.

"Fine, I should be able to graduate soon," I say smugly, thinking of the disbelief on my tutor's face when he read my results.

"That's nice darling." Her voice is distracted, and I can hear her tinkering with things in the background.

"I'm also thinking of piercing my nipple, maybe both, and then chaining them together."

"Hmm, whatever you think." Her voice is far away, and it's obvious she's not paying attention. My lips twist, she doesn't mean to be ignorant, but when she's working, she's miles away.

"What's up?" I ask in a defeated tone.

"Hmm, oh! Me and your father will be working late tonight."

I snort, when don't they? I don't mean to be pissy. I know they have important jobs and I'm busy too; trying to beat Effie to see who can graduate first.

"Okay." My chipper reply is forced. It's strange; for the first year on board, I was so angry with them for pulling me away from my friends and boyfriend and well -- Earth. Now that I've grown up a bit, I can understand why, I just miss spending time with them.

"Could you bring us some cake? Your dad is whining for some." I can hear the smile in her voice and my dad shouting a reply in the background. I smile, despite the loneliness in me.

"Sure, be right there." At least I will get to see them today, maybe I can get them to pay attention for long enough to tell them about my application approval to join flight training once I graduate. Grinning, I imagine their reaction. They will be so proud; my dad's chest will puff up and he will say something stupid like, "I never doubted you." My mum will hug me and tell me how proud of me she is. The youngest pilot ever recorded, that's my aim at least.

"Thanks, honey." Her voice is distracted again. I cut off the comms and grab some cake, putting it on a plate with a lid over it. I don't bother grabbing my jacket, the ship has been warmer than normal lately, so my basic white t-shirt and cargo pants, the cool ones with all the pockets, will be fine. I place my hand on the release scanner at the door to our private housing area and make my way to the labs.

When they first told me I would be coming to space, I imagined the ship to be tiny and cramped. It's the complete opposite. The hallways are well lit and massive, bigger than my old school. The ship has its own swimming pool, theatre, dining areas, the labs and then housing. It's split up into sections: upper, middle and lower. Original, I know. Upper is for crew only, the middle is where I am, it's for the scientists and high up civvies. Lower is for the rest. Under the lower is the storage areas and I'm not sure what else. I suppose it has to be big, we are a colony mission after all; on our way to a new frontier -- Ayama.

The colony has already been started there, and we are the third trip. Only the best of the best get to go; a fresh start the government said. I should have expected my mum and dad to get picked, but it was still a shock when they sat down and told me. And the tests? Ugh. Every medical, psychological, and physical test you can imagine. Plus they tested my skills, intelligence, and what I wanted to do. That test was the longest, sitting down with a shrink and debating the pros and cons of each job and then explaining why I choose that particular field? Not fun.

The journey is supposed to take five years, plenty of time for me to graduate and earn my pilots license. Then, at least when we get to Ayama, I won't be stuck on the ground doing some menial job, not that there's anything wrong with that, but I crave excitement, always have. My mother says I'm an adrenaline junkie, my dad says I take after him. He's a mechanic's son, he studied engineering at the university where my mother was studying. They met in their first year and fell in love. The rest is history, as they say. My mother worked her way up, as did my father.

I smile and nod at people as I pass, they nod back with friendly smiles. Everyone around here knows me. My mother runs the labs and my father is one of the head engineers for the ship. My eye is caught by a flash of black. I notice a few guards standing around talking. I make eye contact with one; he's tall. He's probably a couple of years older than me and just filling out from his growth spurt. His eyes are what stop me though, grey. Unusual. His skin is a dark tan, not from sunlight, not up here, so it must be his natural skin tone. His hair is short and black, so dark it almost blends into the usual guard's uniform. He turns away from me as someone nudges him.

Carrying on, I look in the labs as I pass. It's one thing I enjoy about space, people from all over the world got picked to go. The opportunity to learn new languages and meet new cultures was the only thing I looked forward to.

My mum's lab is at the very end. It's basically a giant square and runs the whole length of the end of the ship. I can see the airlock door up ahead, apparently, it's for the lab's safety, in case any part of the hallway is compromised. I stop when an alarm I've never heard before blares to life. The ship rocks, throwing me into the wall; that's not supposed to happen. I run my eyes around, the guards are running down the corridor towards me.

"Explosion in the main lab." The speaker blares to life, the automation voice is loud to be heard over the siren. Wait, main lab? No!

I whirl to my mum's lab and run, the guards behind me. A panic like I've never known hits me. I sprint faster, pumping my arms the last few feet, my eyes honing in on the door. I'm driven totally by instinct.

I skid to a stop outside the door and try the scanner. It blinks red. I slam my hand down, again and again, trying to see through the glass.

"Come on!" I shout desperately. If I can just get the door open, I can get them out.

A bang on the glass has me freezing, my hand still on the cushioned scanner. My mum's face appears. I'm the spitting image of her, apart from my eyes which I get from my father. Her long brown hair is tied on top of her head. Heart shaped face, with brown eyes staring back at me. Tears are rolling down her face, and I start to panic even more. My mother doesn't cry. She's the strongest person I know. The day I came home with a broken arm from Tommy pushing me off the slide, she sat me down and talked me through the pain in a logical way. She told me to never let anyone see that they get to me. My first heartbreak, my grandad dying, our blowout when I refused to come to space. Nothing, she keeps her emotions in check and thinks logically, unlike me.

I watch as the tears drip down her face, each one a blow to my racing heart. The guards are shouting behind me. I ignore everything as I look into my mother's hopeless eyes. A bang sounds from somewhere in the room making her flinch, but she doesn't turn around. Looking behind her, I scream when I spot my father's crumpled form on the floor. She steps in my way, blocking my view of him and puts her hand on the glass, a sad smile on her beautiful face.

"I'm sorry, baby." Her voice is muffled by the layers of steel and glass between us.

No, no, no. Shaking my head, I smash my palm again and again on the scanner only for it to blink red each time. Frustration burns through me, fighting with the panic clawing at my throat.

"Indy."

I ignore her and the guards, as I try and get through the door. I could circumvent the scanner, but that would take time I don't have. I could kill the circuit board with a-

"Indy, look at me." The voice is stern, the one she uses when I'm in trouble. I freeze and do as I'm told for once in my life, my eyes reluctantly dragging back to hers, as if not looking will make it okay.

"I love you, baby. Be brave and always look for the truth. I'm so proud of you." I put my palm over the glass mirroring hers, each word hammering home my heartbreak. My chest tightens as my heart struggles to beat, the pain indescribable.

No, she can't be saying goodbye. The tears finally burst from my overfilling eyes like a waterfall as a strained sob emerges. Someone grabs me and drags me away from the door. I fight them kicking and screaming, trying to get back to her.

She stays there watching me, the tears dripping steadily down her face. That horrible smile twisting her lips as she faces death. Something explodes behind her making her cringe, but even then, she doesn't look away. Her eyes tighten, and her lips start to turn blue, her shallow breaths puffing against the glass. I keep fighting, needing to be there, needing to save her.

She starts gasping for breath and I fight harder. I hear a grunt behind me and the arms holding me loosen. I jump forward, running back to her. I'm tackled again and lifted in the air. I kick and fight as I watch her suffocate, her eyes dim, and she slumps against the door as I scream.

The noise of the guards, the siren, and everyone else starts to blur together. I'm turned into a chest, a broad one. I notice the name Barrott stitched onto the guard uniform before my head is gently pressed to it.

"Don't look." The deep voice warns from above me.

I try and fight, bashing my fists against his chest. He lets me as sobs rack my body. He doesn't speak or fight back, just lets me pummel his chest until I'm out of energy. I slip to the floor, him following, still cushioning me. Looking into his face through tear-filled eyes, I realise it's the guard from earlier.

"No," I whisper as his face fills with sorrow.

"I'm so sorry."

"No!" I shout it and turn to the door, he allows me this time. The guards are surrounding it, all with grim expressions. One is shouting into the control panel.

"Tell me how this happened!"

"I don't care, keep the door sealed."

I ignore them all. Instead, I look at my mother's body against the glass. I know she's dead, so is my dad. It's now just me. I'm alone in space.

"Not alone." The chest vibrates against me as he speaks.

I don't remember saying it out loud, but I must have because Barrott answers. I ignore him and everyone around me, staring at my mother's open dull eyes.

Eventually, I'm taken away. Barrott lifts me in his arms and strides down the ship. I don't care. I don't care where we are going or who he is. My mind is numb, and I can't feel my body. I know this is shock and I should be bothered, but I let the numbness fill me up.

I'm taken to the medical wing where they check me over. The doctor tries to talk to me, but I ignore him, so he turns to Barrott instead. My eyes lock on the floor replaying my mum's last moments again and again.

Barrott crouches by my side where I sit on a cot. I pay no attention to him, I can see his mouth moving out of the corner of my eye, but it seems like a lot of effort to focus on the words. *I wonder what happened to the cake I was carrying,* I think idly.

Eventually, Effie comes in and throws herself around me sobbing. I don't even try to return the embrace, my arms like lead at my side. She cries into my shoulder, her words floating over my head. Her father, Howard, stands in the curtain door hesitating, heartbreak on his face. He's just lost his best friend. I know the feeling.

The next couple of days are a blur. I don't sleep much, Effie takes me to their housing unit and stays by my side the whole time, assuring me she's there for me. Howard tells me not to worry about anything, that they will look after me. They tell me how sorry they are all the time. I hate the sympathy and pity in their voices.

It's the day of the funeral, if that's what you want to call it. I stand in front of the wooden boxes containing my mother and father. My emotions are fighting the numbness, but I need it now more than ever. The whole ship is here; the first two deaths ever recorded in space. Some are being nosey, some are crying, and some just want to see the orphan girl break down.

I won't. I won't show everyone that. I catch Barrott's eyes where he stands to the side watching me, but I ignore him too. I won't let anyone know how much I'm suffering. How could they possibly understand? I won't let them think I'm the broken girl, when in reality my heart is with the two wooden boxes being pushed into the airlock.

They can't keep the bodies on board, one of the doctors told me, so they will be purged into space. I was told I didn't want to see the remains, I agreed. Now, two coffins fill the hold, both at ceremoniously on separate platforms built into runners which lead to the airlock. There was a ceremony where my mum and dad's colleagues spoke. I didn't listen to a word. None of it matters.

The buzz of the airlock closing sends a stab through my heart, but I block it out. I watch as the outer door opens, and they fly out into the abyss of space. A lone tear rolls down my cheek and I swipe it away before it can fall. I push back the tears by gouging my nails into my thigh, they will be the last ones to fall in front of anyone. I stand there until the crowd breaks, going back to their own lives, and their own families.

I stand there alone on that platform until a throat is cleared behind me. I turn slowly. Barrott is watching me, concern and something else in his eyes. Still not bothering to speak, I watch him, his eyes are sad and filled with concern and he doesn't even shift under my gaze. Eventually he sighs.

"Come on, I'll take you to the Jenkins' quarters. That's where you are living now right?" He winces at his words. I step towards him, and I can see Effie and Howard hesitating at the door, waiting for me. I won't be going with them. I need to be alone with my grief. I need to be somewhere I can break down, somewhere filled with my family.

I shake my head.

"No. I'm staying in my family's unit." I ignore his protests and walk through the whispering people who stayed behind to watch. I hold my head high and walk through, ignoring their stares and remarks. I meet the eyes of a bald man standing next to a woman with jet black hair. They nod at me. Striding through, I count the steps back to my unit. Back to my empty house and life. Only then will I break down and let myself feel. I will be like my mother, I will not show them anything. They will never have it to use against me.

CHAPTER TWO

PRESENT DAY

THERE'S a fifty-fifty chance I can make this corner. Cain is even with me but slows as he approaches it. Grinning, I speed up. The car I'm in purrs with the speed, well they aren't really cars. They are high-tech speeders made for travel on Ayama. There are eight of them in total on the ship, and six of them are in the races. Honestly, I have no idea how Lee managed to get the races and the speeders started without the guards or uppers caring. My guess is he greased some palms. He has his own mechanics as well, so the damage to the speeders is fixed immediately, readying them for when we reach Ayama.

The speeder I'm in flashes a warning. They aren't made for the speeds in which we drive, but Lee managed to bypass the security system and boost them. I don't understand half of it, but driving them? That I can do.

The track runs across the entirety of the two bottom floors of the ship, and no one but the racers and crowd come down here. It's Lee's territory, everyone knows it. They just don't talk about it with everything that's happening. The track is filled with obstacles, tight turns, and jumps. Just about everything you don't want to do in a speeder made for space on a spaceship hurtling towards a planet. But who cares? The adrenaline is amazing and it's the only place I can forget for a while. Plus, the credits, which is the new form of currency, after all, money is outdated and archaic when travelling through space, help Howard. He doesn't question where they come from, he needs them too badly and he doesn't tell Effie. I keep her from this side of me - she worries enough about me as it is. She's too nice and has too big of a heart.

Some call me crazy, I say I'm just an adrenaline junkie. Lee says I accelerate when I should brake, but that's why I win. I ignore the cheering crowd as everything narrows to me and this corner. I switch gears last minute and ignore the beeping from the control panel. My heart races and my hands are clenched on the wheel, the thrill is amazing.

My adrenaline is rocketing, and nerves have no place here, so I grin as I twist the wheel. I hear the screams of the crowd as they expect me to flip and burn. I just manage to make the corner, two of the wheels lifting from the track, but I even out. I look back to see Cain a couple of feet behind me and I laugh, knowing I've won and that he is going to hate it. I rush across the finish line, my adrenaline still racing through my body. Pulling my helmet off, I jump out of the speeder. The crowd goes wild, screams mixing with chants. I simply grin and make my way to Lee. He rolls his brown eyes at me, but I can see the hungry gleam in them. I'm his money maker and he knows it, he never bets against me. Cain has only beaten me once and that was because I was distracted by seeing Barrott in the crowd.

"Transferring the credits to the usual?" He drawls, running his hand through his perfectly styled black hair. I roll my eyes this time. He knows the deal. He's always hoping I'll get greedy and take them for myself - it would mean he has a handle on me.

"Yep," I pop the 'P' and grin at him, the win still riding me. His jumpsuit frames his lean body, but he can't be much taller than me. I wait for him to nod before I start to walk away.

"That was a big risk out there. You're taking more and more. I don't want dead bodies on my track - they attract the wrong kind of attention." He shouts to be heard over the crowd, his southern accent falling away.

I go to answer when a horn sounds, drowning out the crowd and causing everyone to panic. I groan and lean against the nearest speeder, waiting for Barrott's stormy face to make his way to me. Lee mutters and heads over to the guards making their way through the crowd, probably to pay them off.

I spot Barrott's tall form at the front of the guards. His body now fills out the guard uniform, it's like a second skin on him. He has no idea how attractive he is, and I hate him for it. His face is all clean, sharp lines apart from his ever-present stubble. It makes him look ruggedly handsome instead of too perfect to look at. He looks around at the other officers who are rounding up people and then makes a beeline for me.

Cain wanders past me, whispering in my ear as he goes, not the least bit bothered about Barrott bearing down on us, or the fury clearly etched on his face.

"Catch you later, speed demon," he chuckles as Barrott scowls at him. Barrott stops in front of me and waits for Cain to swagger off. I watch him go, his lithe, muscular body showcased in his tight clothes. His ear length brown hair catches the light, almost making a halo appear around it.

"Indy," Barrott starts, a warning in his voice. I hold my hands out with a smirk on my face, but my stomach flips at my name on his lips. It's freaking annoying. That's why I try and stay away from him; not that he lets me.

"Cuff me or don't, but can we skip the lecture?" I keep my smirk in place, knowing it will anger him further. It's my favourite game: see how much Barrott can take before he explodes.

He grabs his hair and yanks. Looking around, he quickly turns and grabs my arm, pulling me behind him. He pushes through the crowd and doesn't stop until we are in an empty maintenance hall. Somewhere deep, and I mean real deep, my heart warms for his concern. No matter how much trouble I get into, he's always there. I know he's always a pace behind me, watching my back; it's the reason why that rubs me the wrong way. I hate that I'm attracted to him and, he sees me as nothing but a responsibility, like a kid sister. He stands in front of me, arms crossed over his barrel chest, one eyebrow raised. I lean back against the wall, knowing he needs to rant before he will let me go.

When my parents died, Barrott decided to take me under his wing. He started treating me like a kid, and it's annoying because he's only two years older than me. As I worked on trying to forget, he worked his way up the ladder, and now he's a lieutenant of the guards. He told me once he did it so he could keep a better eye on me and get me out of trouble. Effie thinks its sweet, I told her it's about as sweet as a turd hitting you in the face.

"Why do we have to do this?" he gripes, his grey eyes laser into me. He knows I race, all the guards know what happens below, but they have bigger issues at the moment. However, they do bust them up every now and again as a show of force. Barrott usually makes a point to sit in the crowd where I can see him. I sometimes slip away before he notices, I guess today is not one of those days.

"Yes, why do we? Can't you just leave me be?" I groan. His eyes soften, but his posture doesn't.

"You know why Indy, someone's got to look out for you." I grind my teeth. "That was a stupid risk out there." He says sternly, the softness disappearing in an instant, making me question if it was ever there.

I step into his space and ignore the flash in his eyes.

"Barrott, you need to stop this. I don't know what messed up sense of protection you claim. I am an adult, I can look after myself." I go to walk around him, and his arm shoots out, blocking my path.

"I know you're an adult Indy, but everyone needs someone. You might think no one cares since..." his voice trails off, knowing it won't end well if he says their names "but I do. So, you can push me away all you want and keep up the attitude, but know that every stupid thing you do, every risk you take, I'll be there, frowning behind you."

I stand there, waiting for his arm to drop, while he waits for my response. He won't get one, we both know that. I stand there breathing in his clean, fresh scent, trying to not betray my reaction to his words. Maybe it's because I know he claims he will be there that I push him away, so I push harder and harder seeing how long it takes for him to walk away. Because everyone leaves eventually, first my mum and dad then dickhead.

He's not joking about everywhere either. When I found my last boyfriend, the cum bubble who was cheating on me, Barrott watched as I punched him in the face and then stormed off. The next day that massive thunder cunt turned up with a fractured wrist and two black eyes - oh and a strange aversion to Barrott. Wonder what happened there? I roll my eyes. Or the time I tried to avoid everyone on my birthday and get shit faced with some randoms. He turned up and carried me home and then held my hair as I vomited. He stayed most of the night, holding me as I drunkenly cried about how much I missed my parents. I woke up in my bed with a present and card next to me and his scent wrapped around me. Not to mention how proud he is when telling everyone about my flight training and scores.

"Okay, come on, Indy. I'll walk you back." His voice is disappointed. It sends a pang through my chest, but I don't let it show.

I wait for his arm to drop and then walk by his side back to my housing unit. It's large; it's a family one after all. But there's no one else who needs it and I refuse to stay with Effie and Howard, no matter how much I love them. I like being surrounded by my parent's stuff and reminded about the good times. It's my own form of personal torture.

We don't talk along the way, he says 'hi' to fellow guards and smiles at people whereas I'm grumpy and withdrawn, imagining how I can slip away before he notices, so I don't have to have the awkward talk with him at my door. Honestly, I just need to not be around him with my attraction to him growing. Two giggling girls stop us and start talking to him. My heart clenches at their flirting and his smile for them - it's so different than the one he uses with me. It does seem more friendly than anything, but I hate it. While he's distracted trying to get them to move, I slip around them and march back to my unit. I'm locked inside by the time he turns up, and I watch through the camera as he stands outside.

"Let me in Indy, we need to talk." I ignore him and watch as he yanks on his hair again. He's going to go bald at this rate.

"I'm not leaving until you let me in, I really do need to talk to you," his voice is stern, but I just stand and watch him, unable to move away. He looks up at the camera and raises an eyebrow at me.

"Fine."

He slides down the side of the door and sits there with his legs outstretched; waiting. He'll be waiting all night. I slide down on my side and stare at the empty space that is my home. My mother's usual warmth and my dad's laugh don't even echo here anymore. Their things are thrown where they had them last. I can't bring myself to move them. I know I won't sleep tonight without seeing her dead face, so I sit there and let their memories cocoon me. I must fall asleep there because a noise startles me awake. The door slides open and I'm in someone's arms before I can move.

"Stop," I grumble.

He ignores me as I try and fight my exhaustion. In all honesty, it's been two days since I last slept, so it's hard. Barrott's arms surround me, making me feel safe as I fight against his warmth.

"Sleep," he commands.

His voice lulls me to fall into a dreamless sleep for once, and the last thing I remember is him kissing my forehead as he places me in my bed.

CHAPTER THREE

DAY 912

FLIGHT TRAINING TODAY WAS AMAZING, I got to take one of the flyers out for a spin with my instructor. There's only six of us in the class, I'm the only one below thirty, oh and a girl. It's an exclusive programme meant to select only a few to train in case of an emergency and for when we get to Ayama. You can either stay there and continue to be a pilot or go back with the ship as part of the flight crew. I've already made up my mind to go back. I haven't told anyone yet because I know it will break their hearts. The idea of a new start on the planet meant for me, my mum, and my father is a no go. I don't belong there anymore, and it wouldn't be a fresh start; I'd be alone. Howard and Effie would live together while Effie finishes her medical training. I know I could live with them, but it seems wrong. Barrott will be busy fitting into the army on the ground and won't have time for me anymore. No, it's better for everyone that I don't drag them down. They need this, and they don't need me there as a reminder of everything that went wrong.

I'm on my way to one of the dining rooms; it's the one we usually use. The other is for the crew and the guards. I step through the door to the noise of the loud crowd ready for dinner time. I start walking to our usual table, and halfway through the crowd, I spot Effie already there with two trays. That girl. I shake my head and smile. A body moves, blocking my view, and I look up to see Cain. I don't have to look far, I'm in no way small. In fact,

I tower over most girls here. It also doesn't help that my curvy body is easy to spot with my double d's. Honestly, my ex told me I looked like a porn star, but I just think I look out of proportion.

Cain is smiling his sinful smile at me. Light blonde hair is swept across his forehead in a rough style, it's obvious he just got up and didn't brush it. His baby blue eyes ooze his charm. It doesn't help that he has an amazing body - all lean muscle. You have to be fit for space and Cain certainly is that. His eyes heat with the knowledge that only someone who has tasted you can get. Bastard, one drunken night I kissed him, and he never lets me forget. He really is insufferable; attitude and charm bigger than life. I let my face fall into its bored mask.

"What?" I ask.

"So, you got escorted home last night. If you wanted to play, you should have come to me, not that stiff." He winks at me. Ugh. I know Barrott knows we kissed, he did find us after all. Not that it bothered him, but Cain teases me about the overprotective man all the time.

"Nah, I like my men, well...men. Not boys," I walk around him, and his laughter follows me.

"Sure. We are inevitable Indy, you'll see."

Jerk. I look up and spot a strawberry blonde head now at our table. I barely control my sigh as I trudge over.

Effie looks up at me in relief as I stand over our table, the girl is too nice for her own good. I look at the vindictive bitch who sits opposite her, no doubt tearing into Effie. She was the one piss-flaps cheated on me with, and she made it very obvious the only reason she did it was to try and hurt me. I look her over, she cut her basic t-shirt into a crop top and is probably wearing shorts or something crazy. Her hair is perfectly styled and her makeup flaw-less. Seriously who has the time for that in space? I arch my eyebrow, my eyes trained on her.

She only comes up to my shoulders and her body looks like a child, that's what makes her jealous, according to Effie. Her dyed hair is going brown at the roots and I almost laugh. My own hair is messy around my head. It starts out brown, then red and blonde highlights towards the bottom. The difference? Mine is natural.

"What do you want Chrissy?" I ask as she plays with her hair.

She frowns, her perfectly painted lips pursing at me. "It's Christina," she says snottily, making me snort.

"Since when?" I scoff.

She flips her hair over her shoulder, her eyes turning menacing. I wish Effie would just let me bitch slap her. "Anyway, I'm just here to talk to Effie about me maybe tutoring her, she is struggling after all."

I laugh, I can't help it. What she means is she wants Effie to tutor her. She's useless. No one knows why she picked medicine; she doesn't have the intellect, patience or stomach. Effie is at the top of her class and due for early graduation. I flash my teeth at her.

"Sure. Now piss off," I grunt, already done with her. She narrows her eyes at me.

"You know, Indy, you could really use a look in the mirror in the morning. I mean, it's embarrassing really." Her voice is snotty again. I don't bother looking down, I know my shirt is creased and my jeans have rips in them from climbing about in the flyers. I don't care. I just stare at her and she flounces up.

"Maybe if you had a mum, you would have some fashion sense."

Oh, fuck no. I barely control my anger, I clench my fists at my side.

I won't react, I won't react, I won't react.

I chant it like a mantra in my head. I can't let her know how much her barb hurts. I try not to give a shit what she says to me. She waits, and when I don't say anything, she turns to Effie.

"I could help you, Effie, God knows you need it, with your grunt of a father."

Nope. Talk shit about me and I don't care, but mention Howard and Effie? I shake my head and lean over towards her.

"I was considering insulting you, but I remembered that I would have to explain it to you after. So, I'll make myself clear in another way," I grab the bowl sitting on the table and tip it over her perfect head. I lean back and watch as she shrieks like a banshee, the red sauce running down her face and onto her crisp white shirt. I've been wanting to do something like that forever. I smirk as Effie doubles over in laughter.

"Chrissy," she ignores me, screeching about her clothes. I can see people looking, but I don't care.

"Chrissy," I say louder. She looks at me and glares, starting up with what will probably be a threat, but I cut her off.

"You ever mention Howard and Effie again and I will destroy you," I let my voice go cold to show her I mean it. She stops and stares at me, her face paling.

"Now, you should get back to your Malibu dream house. It misses you," I say, sitting down next to Effie. She stomps off, sauce dripping as she goes.

"Oh my god." Effie is bent over the table laughing. I sit and watch her, a small smile on my lips. I meant my threat; I would do anything for this girl and her father. No matter how much I push them, they never leave. Howard pretty much adopted me as much as I would allow, and even after dragging himself home after a ridiculously long shift, he still makes time for me. I hear clapping and turn to the table next to us. Two men are sitting there, one in a black shirt, one in a white. Their shoulders are broad, and they are clearly brothers.

One has brown wavy hair and an open looking face; he's handsome. I look to his left, his brother has blonde hair and his eyes twinkle with laughter, his mouth smiling. They both look like cover models from Earth magazines. They must be transfers from the upper decks or lower. They are both clapping and smiling widely at me. I offer them a smile and turn back to Effie. Chairs scrape and then the brothers plop down on our table, avoiding the side where the sauce is.

"That was amazing," the brown haired one gushes, his voice is soft and smooth. His brother nods.

"I wish I had filmed it," the blonde haired one joins in, his voice is deeper than his brother's, it reminds me of those voiceover voices. One that you could get lost in.

I tilt my head at them. "Thanks, you are?" I ask.

The blonde haired one leans over, offering me his hand. He is still smiling, and I wonder if he ever stops; he seems way too happy.

"I'm Eldon." I shake his hand. His face is all sharp angles and his eyes are a deep brown. His brother snatches my hand and shakes it.

"And I'm Auden." His eyes are the same brown as his brother's. I take my hand back gently and jerk my head to Effie.

"That's Effie, I'm Indy." Their smiles widen. They nod at Effie who is staring at them like she's never seen a man before.

"Nice to meet you."

I offer them a small smile.

"Where are you from?" Effie bursts out then covers her mouth with her hand. They smile softly at her.

"What she means is, we haven't seen you around. You uppers or lowers?" Their eyes sparkle with mischief.

"Does it matter?" Auden asks.

"Guess not," I lean back in my chair and watch Effie turn red from her outburst. Poor girl, she can take charge in an emergency and operate on people, but she's lost when talking to boys.

"You a pilot?" he nods at the patch on my shirt and I grin freely.

"Trainee." They both look impressed. "Effie is a healer trainee." She nods along mutely.

"So, brain and beauty," Eldon says looking at me. Auden winks at me.

"Smooth, how many times did you practice that line?" I ask smugly. They both laugh.

"Not working huh?" Eldon asks. I shrug.

"I've heard better, try again?" I see the challenge in his eyes and I know mine reflect it.

"How about: I'm not a photographer, but I can picture me and you together." Auden wiggles his brows suggestively at me. I hold in my smile by biting my lip, that was terrible.

"No? Okay, how about: do you know what my shirt is made of? Boyfriend material!" I do smile at this; their banter is as contagious as is their smiles. Effie is practically a puddle of goo watching them.

"Do those ever work?" I flick my eyes between them.

"You tell us," Eldon says with a flirty smile. I pretend to think about it.

"I don't know, they seem a bit cheesy," I smirk.

"It got you smiling though." Auden high fives his brother.

"And what a smile it is." Eldon winks at me. My smile grows until a hand lands on my shoulder. I groan and lean my head back to meet Barrott's eyes.

"What?" I say bitchily.

"Dumping a bowl on her, really?" I can tell he's trying to be stern, but his lips are twitching.

"Yup. Problem?" I fake innocent and smile sweetly at him. He grins at it.

"No." His voice is soft like his eyes. He looks up, his eyes harden, and his smile disappears.

"Who are you?" I roll my eyes. Two seconds, two whole seconds he was normal. It's a record. I look back at Eldon and Auden. They glance from him to me, still smiling.

"Hi, we are Indy's new musketeers." I groan at Auden's words. It's cute how they speak for each other though.

"That right?" He says with a look at me. I offer him a shrug.

"How did training go?" His voice is his 'answer me now' one.

"Fine," I mutter. He stares at me before looking up. I can see his jaw grinding.

"Okay. I'll swing by your unit later. I better not catch you

22

racing tonight." He nods to Effie and walks off. I don't know why he's even in here, guards eat in the other dining room.

"Who's that?" Eldon asks curiously. Effie leans forward.

"Indy's ever-present bodyguard." She giggles. I slap her arm slightly but don't correct her.

"I knew you were trouble." Auden grins and I find myself grinning back.

"What was that about racing?" Eldon asks, I wink at him.

"Wouldn't you like to know?"

He glances at his brother and then they both look back at me, playfulness on their faces.

"How about a bet? If you win, you can pick a prize. If we win, you have to tell us about the racing." I stare at Auden, my reckless side can't turn down a challenge, and Effie knows it because she groans.

"Bet on what?" I watch them. They stand up and offer me one hand each.

"We'll show you. You coming, Effie?" Eldon's voice suppresses my questions. I stand, ignoring their hands and Effie and I follow them out.

TRANSMISSION LOG 00302
DATE: 2033
MISSION: 43, COLONY
SHIP: DAWNBREAKER
DESTINATION: AYAMA

>............. Accepted
> The rebel attacks have gotten worse. We are
unsure where they are getting their weapons

from. They also sent us a message. "Tell the
ship the truth or else." Please advise on how
to proceed?

THE BROTHERS LEAD us to the lagoon, at this time of the day it's dead. I get the afternoon off luckily, so does Effie. It's one of the perks of graduating early. Auden and Eldon start stripping, and I take a second to appreciate their bodies; slim, but packed with muscle. They both have an eight pack, and that delicious V shown by their low riding jeans. I slowly make my way back up to where they are grinning at me. I don't blush, I don't care about being caught checking them out. After all, that's what they wanted. Effie stammers and turns bright red.

"What kind of challenge is this?" She bursts out. I grin, so do the brothers.

"Race you to the wall and back," Auden says.

"There's two of you, how is that fair?" I arch my eyebrow. I'm not above cheating and looking innocent. They consider it seriously.

"You can have a head start."

I smile innocently. Thanks."

They grin again. They don't know I swim laps when I can't sleep. This lagoon is basically a swimming pool, which has a beach into the water and then a wall at the other end. Seats run along the beach as does a small jetty. I had been so impressed when I first saw it.

"You in, or are you scared?" Eldon taunts.

I smile evilly. I slowly pull my top off revealing my lacy white bra. I hear them muttering, and I make sure to make eye contact as I slowly lower my trousers. Standing in nothing but a thong and a lace bra, I wink at the brothers. Their eyes are locked on my body and heating fast. I know I have a nice body, I don't flaunt it but I'm not scared of using it when I need to.

I slowly walk towards them where they stand in front of the jetty. I make sure to sway my hips. At the last minute, I turn and sprint down the jetty calling over my shoulder.

"Ready, set, GO!" I scream the last as I dive in. I instantly start swimming, my competitive nature hard to resist. I can hear their swearing from here. They splash as they enter the water, making me swim harder. I'm about halfway when I feel a tug on my ankle. They both grab one and yank me back. I nearly sputter water as they race past. Oh, game on.

I chase them but their legs and arms are longer and they touch the wall just before me. I end up treading water in the middle of them both, laughing.

"Cheats," I accuse around a laugh.

"Like you aren't," Auden says. He slicks his hair back, and my mouth goes dry, it makes him look so much older.

"Race you back?"

They both nod and we all start swimming. I slow a bit and they keep pace with me. I dunk under and grab onto Auden's arm. He doesn't expect it and goes under as I swim past. Eldon is still going. I try to grab his ankle, he stops and dunks under. They both chase me and take turns pushing me under the water.

It's the most fun I've had in a long time. We all swim back to the beach when we get tired where Effie is laid reading a book. I walk towards her, with my up to no good smile in place. She doesn't even see me coming before I jump on her, drenching her.

"INDY!" She screams and tries to push me off.

I squeeze my hair on her and she screams louder. Someone picks me up and chucks me back in the water, and when I surface, I see Auden and Eldon both with innocent expressions on their face. I smile and then make my way out again. They both watch as water runs down my body, and I can't help but tremble a little at their expressions.

I walk towards a free chair and grab a towel, drying off and trying to ignore them. I end up just putting my shirt back on, for now, still too wet to put my trousers back on. When everyone is dried, we drag the chairs closer and sit in a circle talking.

"So, racing?" Auden asks. I guess they did win, even if they cheated.

"It's down below, we race modded speeders." They both look intrigued, they are definitely adrenaline junkies like me.

"I heard rumours but never-" Eldon whispers. Auden practically bounces on his seat.

"Can we go?" I laugh at his hopeful expression.

"Sure, next time, you can bring Effie." They both nod eagerly, she stares at me in shock.

"I get to come?" She asks hopefully, as I glance at her.

"Yeah, it will be good for you to get out." She smiles softly at me.

"When is it?" Eldon asks mirroring his brother's excitement. I shrug.

"We get a message the morning of." They both nod again.

"So what are we doing now?" They ask in unison, it's cute. Effie heaves up with a sigh.

"Some of us have work. See ya later Indy." She waves at the brothers, and I smile at her retreating form.

"So what are we doing?" Auden wiggles his eyebrows.

"I was going to have a chill afternoon," I say stretching back on the chair.

"Can we join?" Eldon asks. I smile as I look up at the painted sun and blue sky on the ceiling. I pretend to think about it and the next thing I know, one of them is on top of me, shaking out their wet hair. Jumping up with a giggle, I chase after them.

We spend the afternoon at the beach talking, laughing and playing. Effie refused to keep taking bets with me, she said I get too crazy. The brothers have no such qualms, they challenge me all the time, it keeps it interesting. By the end of the day, I owe them a massage each, a cuddle. and a favour of their choosing. Auden owes me a foot rub, the right to call him sweet cheeks for the rest of the week and his dessert for the next three days. Eldon only owes me a favour.

It's strange how comfortable I am around them. I usually get bored of people after an hour or so and I don't tend to let people in. I guess it's nice not to be known as the *orphan*. Their eyes don't hold pity, I hope it stays that way.

That night I'm sitting in my lonely living quarters when the buzzer for the door sounds. I frown and walk towards it. I hope it's Barrott but I also kind of don't. When I look through the camera and see the brothers, I start to panic. They don't know I'm alone! I open the door and block their way.

"Hey guys, what are you doing here?" Auden holds up a bag and then shimmy's past me. Eldon offers me a sweet smile and kisses my cheek as he follows his brother.

"Where's the parentals?" Eldon asks. A throb of pain runs through me which I cover by turning my back on them and using the scanner to close the door,

"Work," I say vaguely.

"Awesome," Auden says and starts dumping the bag's contents on the table. I walk closer, my curiosity getting the better of me, and spot the alcohol. I shake my head with a smile. It's not hard to find up here but it can be pricey.

"What are we doing?" I ask leaning on the chair back. Auden and Eldon give me matching grins.

"We are playing 'never have I ever,' sweetheart." Auden winks at me. I can't help but grin back. Their personalities are already filling up the empty space, the cold space warms for the first time in a year. I pull out the chair and sit down, trying to stay in the moment.

"Let's do it." They turn to each other.

"Told you she would," Auden says. Eldon rolls his eyes and then winks at me. He goes and grabs cups and sits down opposite me. Auden sits down next to him and shows me the three bottles.

"Ladies choice." I grab the bottle of whiskey and a cup. Eldon grabs his chest dramatically.

"I think I'm in love." His voice is dreamy. I flip him off and start pouring.

"Never have I ever stolen anything," Eldon declares, I take a sip and their shocked faces look back at me. I smirk. If they thought I was some goody two shoes, they were wrong.

"Whaaa-"Auden drags on. I lean back.

"What did you steal?" Eldon asks.

"That's not part of the game," I remind.

"Come on beautiful, spill." I look at Auden.

"Beautiful, really?" I smile.

"Stunning?" Eldon chimes in.

"Sexy?" Auden adds.

"Ravishing?" Eldon shouts louder.

"Good looking?" Auden shouts over him. I can't help it, I laugh hard, my smile wide enough to make my cheeks ache. Eldon nods.

"I like that one. So, good looking, spill." They both look so eager.

"Fine, if you get to call me that I'm going to call you..." I trail off tapping my chin. They both lean forward eager.

"Pretty?" I suggest. They look disgusted.

"Handsome?" I offer. Eldon nods. I look at Auden and wink.

"Cutie." He smiles, flashing me dimples I didn't know he had. Holy space balls.

"Okay, but you still need to tell us."

I groan in mock frustration. "Fine. I stole a bike on Earth." Their jaws drop.

"As in a motorbike?" Auden asks incredulously.

"Yup, cutie." I take a sip and watch.

"From who?"

"My shit stick of a next-door neighbour. I took it for a joy ride and then left it on his front garden covered in mud."

They both laugh.

"Never have I ever been in love," Auden says watching me closely. I don't sip.

"Really?" Eldon asks. He sounds hopeful. I shrug one shoulder.

"There was a guy on Earth. If I stayed, I could see myself loving him, I was already halfway there." I'm honest with them. They flick a look at each other but I decide to carry on the game.

"Never have I ever space walked." The game goes on like that and before it finishes, we are all a bit tipsy. I tell them they can sleep here tonight on the couch if they want. They ask if my parentals will mind, I just smile and say no.

It's nice having someone else here. I fall asleep with a smile on my face, the whisky heating my blood.

CHAPTER FOUR

DAY 913

"HEY GOOD LOOKING, what's Indy short for?" Eldon asks as we walk towards the dining room for breakfast. Each brother is on a side of me, walking so close our hands brush. I pointedly ignore the tingles that each touch causes.

"Nothing. My mum named me after some astronomy software. Ironic right?" I snort. They hum their agreement. We carry on walking, slowly getting closer to one another until both of my arms feel like they have been stuck in a plug socket.

Grief is strange. You can be okay one minute and the next you're a wreck. Some days I can push it to the back of my mind and forget about it, some days it just hits you in the face. Time lessens it, but the pain is still there, and the smallest things can trigger you. Seeing the mother with her arm wrapped around her kid laughing as they walk by is a big one. The pain hits me, I choke it down and force a smile at the brother's banter. I look at the floor, concentrating on walking and breathing, the pain bubbling like a volcano ready to erupt. I run into something hard and look up. Both brothers are standing in front of me, blocking my way with a frown. I force a smile, although I'm betting it's more a grimace.

"What's up?" My voice is strained, but it's the best I can do. I usually hide away when this happens, give myself some time to deal with it. Then I bottle it back up and move on like nothing happened. Eldon lifts his eyebrow at me.

"I was just going to ask you that?"

I look anywhere but at their faces.

"Nothing, let's get some food." I try to step around them, but Auden blocks me. I stop and glare at the floor. Can't they just leave me be?

"Good looking, what's going on?" Auden's voice is soft and filled with worry.

"What do you mean?" I mutter, staring at their feet. *They have large feet. Okay, concentrate on the shoes, what do they look like, what colour are they?* Eldon steps into me and lifts my chin, stopping my coping mechanism.

"Sweetheart, what's going on?" I start to panic as I can feel the tears coming on. I step back shaking my head, but they don't allow me to go any further. Auden circles to my back and Eldon to my front. My breathing picks up, they can't hug me, I'll break down. I can't do that, no one can know I'm not okay. Eldon lifts his arms and goes to hug me; I panic. I dart around him and sprint back to my unit. Not much rational thinking left, all I know is I need to get away before they find out or make me cry.

I make it back and lock the door, my breathing heavy. I look up into the camera when I have my breathing under control. They are both standing there, looking confused at the door.

"Indy, let us in. What's wrong?" Auden sounds distressed and his face is crestfallen.

"Did we do something?" Eldon asks, sadness in his voice.

I back away and sit on the floor, my knees to my chest with my arms wrapped around them as the tears start to fall. Why do they have to be so kind? Why can't they see I just need to be alone? They are whispering to each other, but I ignore them and start counting. Sometime after my third breakdown, I realised concentrating on something helped me push the feelings back. Counting is the best I can find. When I reach thirty, they look back at the camera.

"Okay Indy, we will leave you alone for now. We will be at breakfast if you want to join us. If not, we will see you for the evening meal?" Eldon asks. He's rubbing his head like it hurts. He ends it on a question, but I don't respond. Auden and Eldon look so sad and rejected, but I don't have anything in me to comfort them yet, not when the grief is so thick I can almost taste it on my tongue. They wave sadly at the camera and turn away. When I can't see them anymore, I release a breath I didn't realise I was holding and carry on counting. It takes to a hundred, better than last time. I stand, go and splash some cold water on my face. I hang my head, well that's fucked. I can't go and see them today, they will ask too many questions.

I feel so raw after that breakdown that I decide to head to flight training early, get some alone time in the simulator. I'll bury my head all day in learning, I'll try and avoid the brothers. With a frown, I stand up. I haven't seen Barrott since yesterday. That's not like him.

I shake my head, I know he can't be around me all the time, but he usually comes and checks on me at least once a night. A pang of irrational jealousy spikes through me. What if he was with someone?

I slowly make my way through the corridors and into the loading bay they use as a flight training centre. I keep my head up, eyes open, looking for the brothers in case I have to dart away. By the time I can see the hangar door, my frown is bigger than ever. With a start, I realise why. I miss Barrott. Fuck that, definitely time for a long day learning about the mechanics of space travel and navigation systems. I lower my head, lost in my own thoughts. I head to the hangar door, but stop when I see Barrott there, his usual frown on his face and his arms crossed. Relief runs through me, then anger. God, I'm a mess today. I ignore him and go to the scanner, he moves and blocks it, forcing me to look at him.

"What?" I put my attitude in my voice, hoping it will fool him. He frowns harder, guess that didn't work.

"You weren't at breakfast."

It's a statement so I wait, not wanting to tell him anything. He steps closer. His scent calms me a bit, pushing the last tendrils of my grief away.

"Everything okay?" His voice is quiet, and his eyes have softened. They search mine with too much intensity, he sees too much. I force a smile.

"Peachy," I lie. His eyes narrow, his radio crackles, but he ignores it. We stand there staring at each other, both unwilling to start.

"Fine, lie to me. I better see you at the evening meal." I frown before I can help it, and a flash of victory crosses his face before I can comment. "I'm working through dinner; some stuff went down last night." I almost sag with the relief that he wasn't with someone, then I realise what I'm doing and glare.

"Fine, like I care."

He just rolls his eyes at my weak lie. Bloody man. He leans closer and kisses my forehead, making my stomach clench and my heart speed up.

"I'll see you later and you will tell me why you look like you've seen a ghost, even if I have to make you." With that, he walks away. Great. I can't help myself, I watch his peachy ass as he walks away, pants clinging to it lovingly. Space balls, am I jealous of his trousers? I need help. I groan and turn back to the hangar door. Scanning my hand, I wait until it flashes green.

The steel door slides open, revealing the large open loading bay. This one is used to store some of the emergency escape flyers. There are a hundred scattered all over the ship. Other than that, the loading bay is clear, it's not in use until we land. They have created a simulator of an old flyer in the corner to practice in, and if you are deemed worthy, you can take out one of the emergency flyers for testing and practice. So far only two people have been allowed to, me and Steve. He thinks because he's older than me that he will be the first to graduate, but he's too cocky. He doesn't respect space and how easily it can take down a flyer. I spent over two weeks pouring over footage from inside flyers and accounts from when they have gone down or nearly gone down. Just to test myself, to see how I would react in the situation. Plus, I have a higher score than him.

I head to the simulator, it will be free at this time. Training doesn't start until 11:00 am and it's only 9:00. Plenty of time to lose myself in space.

Earning the latest high score on the leaderboard on the simulator, I cheer to myself. When I arrived there, Steve had taken over my top three spots. I tried not to get competitive. After all, I hadn't used it in two weeks. With a smirk, I look at the top ten leaderboard scores flashing on the control panel to the left. All me. I even managed to beat my highest record. Beat that Steve. I do a little dance to myself, wiggling in my seat as I shake my hips.

Effie once asked me why I wanted to be a pilot; why would I want to be in charge? I told her I didn't, but why would I want to keep my feet stuck to the ground when I could fly in the air, see the unknown, discover sights that people only dream of? She didn't ask again after that.

The hangar door slides open as the rest of the class enters. Steve's eyes narrow at me and I stick my tongue out before hopping out of the sim and heading to join in.

Today's testing consists of reactions under extreme stress situations. Apart from me, everyone dreads this one. Apparently, I don't react like a normal person. I can push the fear and nerves away, it helps me think clearly and make the decisions without hesitating. Maybe it has something to do with that fact I'm always searching for the next big rush. Who knows? Either way, I excel at it, much to Steve's and the other trainee's, chagrin.

The testing goes on until late afternoon. I was second and passed all three situations the first time. I spend the rest of the training watching the other trainees and their mistakes, so I can make sure I never do it.

Training finishes at 3:30 pm and everyone broke up for lunch. I decided to stay and run some more simulations. I waved at them as they left, and the instructor lifted his eyebrow at me in question. I just grinned at him and opened the flyer door. He grinned and left me to it. They know better than to try and make me take a break when I don't want to.

By the time I look at my watch again, it's 6:00 pm. I debate just going back to my unit, but I know Barrott will just track me down. My stomach takes this time to remind me I haven't eaten all day. *Fine*, I grumble as I close the flyer and let myself out of the hanger.

My mood improved throughout the day and I'm back to my usual sarcastic self. I smile at some people as I pass and when I get to the dining area, the smell hits me, and I groan in hunger. I make my way through the tables and nearly turn back when I see who's at ours.

Effie, Barrott, and both brothers. Bloody hell, it looks like an intervention. Barrott is glaring at his watch and both brothers look antsy, even Effie looks upset. Great. I make my way over and thump my bag down on the table.

"Hey, cuties what's up with the faces?" I ignore the looks and slump in my seat. I can feel Barrott glaring at me and the brothers' questioning looks. I turn to Effie instead and offer her a smile.

"How did the surgery go this morning?" Her face breaks into a winning smile.

"They said I did excellent!" I clap my hands in happiness and smile big at her.

"Knew you would babe! I'm so proud of you." I lean forward and offer her a one-armed hug. When I pull back, I brace, and look at Barrott.

"You're late. I saw your class leaving this afternoon." His voice is accusing, I shrug and look around the busy area.

"I decided to run some more sims," I say casually.

Auden leans forward, "I heard you aced all three tests today, good looking." I wink at him.

"Of course, I did sweet cheeks." He leans over the table and kisses my cheek. Eldon does the same on the other cheek.

"Well done." They both offer me, but I can still see the confusion in their eyes from this morning. I should probably apologise, but then I would have to explain. Instead, I offer them a warm smile.

"Indy," Barrott growls.

"Barrott," I mimic his tone and look back at him. His lips twitch and then he sighs.

"Well done, never doubted you." I smile at him in a peace offering

"So, we still having a movie night tonight, good looking?" Eldon asks. I nod and start on the food on the table, not caring whose it is and that I'm shovelling it down. I'm way too hungry for that. Barrott passes me his dessert without saying anything and carries on eating. I smile down at it, my traitorous heart speeding up again. Even my lady parts perk up.

"Cool, we will come to your unit after we grab a few bits." I nod, still eating. I look at Barrott as he makes a noise. He's glaring at the brothers, something in his face stops me. He looks jealous, but wait, he can't be, right? It's gone before I can ask, and I look back down at my food. His fists are clenched on the table and he stands up abruptly.

"I'll see you tonight then Inds," he says, staring at me.

"Huh?" I ask confused. His eyes are warning me not to argue.

"Like I trust you not to get into trouble, plus, it's my night off." With that, he walks away. I'm left watching him as he dumps his tray and leaves. Wait, Barrott is coming to hang out? What in the planets? I swing my gaze to Effie, a question on my lips. She just smiles at me knowingly. The brothers get my attention again.

"We'll go grab our stuff, see you in a bit," Auden offers. They both smile at me before leaving. I turn back to Effie.

"I told you, that man thinks of you like his girlfriend," she gushes.

"What?" I choke and drain my cup, my eyes watering.

"Don't play stupid. He turns up to every party, every race, and follows you around, glaring at any man who looks at you for too long." She smiles dreamily as I sputter.

"That's because he thinks I'm some sort of little sister," I defend grumpily, playing with the rest of my uneaten food.

"Hmm, sure whatever you want to think. I've just never seen a 'brother' look at a sister like he's imagining what she looks like naked." My mouth drops open and I turn to her, to see her laughing at me.

"He does not," I grumble. But I wish he would. No damn it, I don't. He's annoying and bossy and hot as hell. Space balls, I'm so screwed up.

"Sure hunny, I can't wait for you two to finally get it on."

I ignore her and eat my food, the thought of Barrott and me together sending pleasure down my spine, not that I'll ever admit it. Effie takes pity on me instead and turns her attention to the brothers. She quizzes me about what happened when she left. I tell her about everything and I'll admit, it feels good. I feel like a normal teenage girl, gossiping about boys.

"So, now you're up to four men interested in you?" She asks giddily. Wait, four? I count in my head.

"How did you get four?" I ask wearily.

"Duh. Barrott: boy has been in love with you for years. Cain: he wants in your panties so bad it's comical. And now Auden and Eldon."

I flap my mouth open and closed.

"Barrott isn't in love with me. Cain is an asshole who I kissed once when I was drunk," I protest, pointing my pudding covered spoon at her. She just smiles at me.

"I'm ignoring your total lack of knowledge on them, so Auden and Eldon." I groan as she tries to dig for gossip.

"I know. They are both so sweet. I love that they don't care how crazy I get." I eat my pudding, smiling at our bets last night.

"I do not envy you." She laughs. "I thought having two men after you was a dream for most girls." She laughs harder and I groan.

"Maybe for most girls, but I'd be quite happy having just one. I can barely manage my own feelings, never mind juggling," I glance at her, "Four."

She smiles at me and then it dims.

"When they came in here this morning, they said you freaked and ran away and wouldn't tell them why." She gives me a knowing look, but doesn't ask. "Those boys are smitten with you, and you hurt them when you blocked them out."

I shrug, unwilling to talk about my freak out. She squeezes my arm where it rests on the table.

"Let someone in Indy, I know you don't want to talk about it, but you are going to have to. Those boys want you to, so lean on them." I stare down at my food.

"What if they leave?" I ask quietly.

"You are too smart for this. They won't leave, they are hooked. You have to give someone a chance Indy, before you turn into a hermit. You might be able to fool some idiots into thinking you're okay with your fake smile, but they see through that. As do Barrott, Cain, and I." I don't answer straight away. I thought I was doing well hiding it from them.

"I've only known them a day," I mumble.

"Some people you can know for a lifetime and never have that kind of bond, or be that comfortable. Others you can know for hours and you just know it's right. Like you've known them forever." It's true, I feel like I've known them so long, how is that possible?

"When did you get so smart?"

"When my best friend broke and decided to close herself off

from the world." Her voice is soft, and full of sadness. I look at her and see the tears swimming in her eyes.

"I didn't just lose them that day Indy, I lost you too. You've never been the same and that's okay, you shouldn't be. But I have to watch as you destroy yourself, taking stupid risk after stupid risk. Closing yourself off from everyone. It hurts, you're like my sister. I miss you."

I want to apologize. I want to let her in, but I can't. I'm just sitting staring at the girl whose heart I broke. I didn't even know I was doing it. I thought I was helping her by not letting her see how damaged I was, but looking into her eyes, now I see that I hurt her even more. Is that really what I'm doing, trying to destroy myself? I think back over the last year and all the stupid stuff I have done. I just wanted to feel alive, but I can imagine how it must look to her. The number of times she's had to patch me up or stand by as I take the risks. I frown. Yeah, I would hate to watch her do that, but I can't change who I am. Not even for her. This new me is who I have to become to survive losing my parents. Maybe I could tone it down a little though, for her? She interrupts my morbid thoughts.

"They might surprise you Indy, let them." With that, she offers me a sympathetic smile and heads home to see her dad. I groan, and look at my food. I just wanted to get by one day at a time, but it looks like that plan is crumbling down around me. What to do? I don't want to see the pity on their faces. I wouldn't trust Cain with this, and Barrott? I sigh again. He knows, and pushes me to let him in, but what if I do and he sees how damaged I really am? No, it's better keeping it to myself. I just hope they let me.

TRANSMISSION LOG 00305
DATE: 2033
MISSION: 43, COLONY
SHIP: DAWNBREAKER

DESTINATION: AYAMA

>............... Accepted
>There was an attack last night in the crew
quarters. They painted their symbol on the
wall. We have managed to keep it from the rest
of the colony but if these attacks continue,
they will soon find out. Guards have heard
rumours of secret meetings between the rebels.
Please advise on how to proceed?

CHAPTER FIVE

DAY 913

THE BROTHERS ARE WAITING outside my unit when I get there, matching smiles on their faces. My brain stops when I see they both have dimples. I'm done for. My smile is instantaneous, my bad mood from my conversation with Effie wiped away. My girly bits perk up again as I eye them. It really isn't fair to be that good looking.

"We buzzed, but the parentals must be out," Auden says happily. My steps falter, but I manage to carry on. It's strange; them not knowing about my parents, I'm so used to everyone just knowing. It's refreshing, but I wonder how long until they find out? I'm not a fool, I know it will be mentioned in passing or they will over-hear, I'm just trying to make the most of the time they don't know. Before that knowing look that people give you comes into their eyes, before they know me as the *orphan girl*, not Indy.

I don't say anything, but scan my hand and let them follow me in. I flounce down on the sofa and watch as they drop their stuff on the floor. I raise my eyebrows at the bags. It sends a pang into my chest, which I quickly push away.

"In case we end up staying again," Eldon says matter of factly. He presses the button on the living room wall, and the holo-screen raises from the floor. Auden lays down next to me, his feet hanging over the back of the sofa and his head in my lap. Eldon turns around and spots his brother. He shakes his head, but comes to sit on my other side.

"Which one of you two is the oldest?" I ask, stroking Auden's hair.

"Guess." He smiles up at me.

"What do I win if I'm right?" They both grin at me when I say that, those evil little dimples flashing at me.

"What do you want?" I ignore the underlying meaning to his words.

"You two have to be my little servants for a day." Auden laughs, but agrees. Eldon's face shutters for a moment, a faraway look coming into his eyes. I frown, and reach out to touch his thigh. He jumps, then looks at me, his happy personality soon returning, and he offers me a small smile. I know about hiding pain, so I pretend I didn't see anything.

"Hmmm, I'd have to say Eldon is the oldest." His smile widens.

"Correct, good looking, only by a year. He got the age, I got the beauty." Auden wiggles his eyebrows at me. I shake my head and continue running my hands through his silky hair. Eldon ignores us and puts on a movie. He leans back and wraps his arm around my shoulders, pulling me to his side.

"So, are you two downers?" I ask. I'm really curious; it's next to never that someone's rank changes.

Auden offers me an unreadable look, he glances at his brother then me again.

"Yeah. Our dad is a mechanic. He got promoted, so we ended up moving up. Lucky us, right?" His voice sounds bitter and holds a warning, about what I'm not sure.

"Don't like downers?" Eldon's voice is stern, and he's turned to stone against me.

"I have no problem with anyone. I think it's stupid how we are divided. The whole point in coming to space and travelling to Ayama was a fresh start. Everyone should have one, no rules and societal expectations defining their limitations," I make sure to stare at Eldon. He turns and looks at me, and whatever he sees on my face softens his.

"Sorry good looking, we are used to being judged. Not everyone up here is happy with our move. I wish you were right." His voice is quiet, but it echoes with hurt.

"Fuck them," my voice is hard and makes him flinch.

"What?" He sounds surprised at my outburst.

"If they don't like it, fuck them. Don't let them know it bothers you, rise above it. They will fall with petty feelings and gossip." My words echo my Mother's and I swallow hard, pushing down the memories. Eldon stares at me, his face serious.

"How do we do that?" He asks it softly, almost afraid.

"Easy. Why do you care what they think? Do you love them? Are they your friends or family? If the answer is no, then it doesn't matter, they don't define your self-worth. Showing them that they don't affect you takes away any power they have over you. And that's what they want, power. It's what it all comes down to. They think they are better, and you letting them get to you offers them validation. It will only eat you up, instead, let it eat them up. You moving up makes them question themselves, so they try and put you down to remain feeling powerful." I turn back to the screen and watch the film. I can feel them both staring at me. Eldon leans down and kisses my cheek.

"You're right, pretty lady. Thank you." I can hear the wonder in his voice but I just shrug, uncomfortable with the praise. Auden leans up and kisses my other cheek.

"She's right, brother. All we need is each other and it seems our Indy doesn't care about rank or credits."

I look at him and see the caring in his eyes. I don't know how to respond, so I choose to ignore them. Eventually, they go back to watching the film, but I feel something shift with our conversation. I only wish I knew what.

Halfway through the film, the door buzzer sounds. I groan, not wanting to get up. Eldon kisses my cheek and jumps up to get it.

Barrott comes in like he owns the place, and ignoring Auden, he sits down where Eldon was. I roll my eyes when he doesn't say anything and just starts watching the movie. What a cock block. Eldon comes back and grins at me, letting me know he's not mad, then he sits down next to his brother. There's a tension in the air that wasn't there before and half an hour later, I excuse myself to go to the bathroom. As I'm coming back, I hear voices, so I stop to listen.

"I don't want to see her hurt is all." I easily recognise Barrott's voice.

"We don't plan on hurting her." Eldon defends.

"Good, she's had enough pain in her life. Oh, and don't bring what happened to her parents up in front of her."

My hearts stop at Barrott's concerned words. I know he's just trying to protect me, but he's done the complete opposite. I stop and wait, my heart in my throat.

"What happened to them?" Auden asks confused. I lean my head against the wall. Couldn't I have just one more night where they didn't know? I hear Barrott's inhale when he realises the mess he's just made. His guilt is palpable, it's the only reason I do what I do next. I step out into the living room and wait for all three to look at me.

"They're dead," I say in a calm voice, my emotions controlled inside. Then I step around the sofa and sit back down, eyes on the screen. I can practically hear the gears in their head as they figure it out. They might not have known me exactly, but they will have heard the stories. They don't say anything and neither do I but, for the rest of the film, my heart is crushed.

Barrott leans into me. "I'm sorry Inds, I didn't…" He stops, and I ignore him. I'm not mad I just don't know what to do.

Barrott leaves after the film, I think he still feels guilty. He kisses my forehead and tells me he will see me tomorrow. I just nod at him. The silence is strained after he leaves.

"Good looking?" Eldon asks. I take a deep breath and turn to them. I don't see pity in their eyes, only understanding, and I'm shocked into silence.

"Why didn't you tell us?" he asks. I shrug, not wanting to open my mouth in case it lets the pain I'm hiding out.

"Is that what this morning-" Auden stops and stares at me in sadness. I start to fidget. I need to get out of here; their sadness is infectious. I go to stand, and Eldon moves to the floor in front of me. He looks up at me through his lashes. He looks so young like that. So vulnerable that I stop and slowly lower myself back down.

"Our dad is an asshole," he lets me see all his pain and suffering as he speaks. I stare at him in confusion. He keeps eye contact with me even as his face burns red. My confident goofy Eldon disappearing to show me a shy ashamed boy.

"He treats us like slaves, we don't classify him as our father. We only have each other." His reaction earlier makes sense and I feel guilty for suggesting he be my servant for a day. "He beats us, not as much anymore because we are too big. But he used to, a lot. He wears this professional version of himself and I hate it. I know the monster within him and no fake smiles and smart words can make up for that. I walk around with these silent scars and I feel like everyone knows, like everyone's judging me." He takes a deep breath.

"You never have, even now I don't see any judgment in you. Just anger on our behalf and that Indy, is one in a million." He's right, my anger is rising. I hate their father and I don't even know him. How could he hurt them like this? How could they turn out so amazing with such a shit parent? The pain and sorrow on their faces only fuels my rage. I go to stand, but he puts his hands on my thighs, trapping me.

"How are you two so happy all the time?" I whisper, needing to know. Auden answers, but I don't look away from Eldon; caught up watching as each expression crosses his beautiful face. They're so raw and honest.

"Not all the world is shit, Indy, just because one person is. We make sure to find the laughter in life. It's the only way to push the darkness back." I look from brother to brother, my resolve to keep them away crumbling like my heart. It aches for their lost childhood and the pain they endured. I look back at Eldon and know he will answer any questions I have, holding nothing back. He would lay his scars bare and suffer through the memories if it would help.

How can he do this? How can he share his pain so freely? I know he's doing it to make me understand; to offer his support. I just don't get how he can sit there, the pain and anger so clear on his face, and offer me his deepest secrets, but something in me softens at him for doing this. We might not have the same lives, and there are things they will never understand about my loss, and things I will never understand about their pain, but we share a common theme. We are all orphans in one way or another.

I lean forward and hug him.

"You are always welcome here," I whisper. Auden shuffles until he sits behind me, wrapping his arms around me and his brother, offers his support in silence.

"It's okay, we don't see him much-"

I stop him with a playful growl. "It's nice having you here. It's so quiet all the time, you two fill it up."

Auden squeezes me harder. "Then you will never get rid of us."

I smile into Eldon's shoulder and let them hold me as the pain runs through us all, and at this moment, it lessens a bit. They didn't run, and they didn't judge, they understand, and it helps.

"Hey, good looking, I hope you know CPR, because you are taking my breath away!"

I groan out a laugh as Eldon shakes with silent laughter in my arms.

"You must be a campfire because you're super hot and I want s'more," Eldon says around a laugh, making me giggle in between them.

They spend the night again. We all lay cuddled on the sofa, me in between them. I hold Auden as he trembles and cries out in his sleep and Eldon holds us both. I understand the way he watches his brother now, always trying to protect him. It's clear Auden still suffers, Eldon too although he tries to hide it. Their breathing eventually evens out and I make a promise to myself then and there that their father will never hurt them again and that if I ever see him, not even Barrott will be able to stop me.

DAY 917

OVER THE NEXT couple of days, we fall into a routine. I go to flight training and then I hang out with Effie during the day, the boys with us. At night, they come to my unit and we talk and laugh. They always stay over. One night, they insisted I go to bed instead of staying curled up on the sofa. I did, but Auden's whimpering woke me, so I crawled into their makeshift bed on the floor and held him.

Barrott keeps his distance and I'll admit, it hurts. I don't know if it's because of the guilt he feels, or if he's busy. Every time I see him, his eye bags are bigger and the lines of exhaustion on his face are wider.

I'm just walking back from training when I spy him leaning against the hall wall with his eyes closed. I step closer and gently shake him. His hand reaches out and grabs my arm, halting my movements. His eyes slit open, and when he sees it's me, he relaxes his grip.

"What are you doing Indy?" Even his voice is tired.

"I could ask you the same thing." I look at his clothes, they are a rumpled mess, it's so unlike him. "You need to sleep," I state sternly, concern lacing my words.

"I will, I'm just on my way there now." His eyes slide shut again. I stare at him before sighing, grabbing his hand, I pull him along.

"What are you doing?" He grumbles, but stumbles after me. I ignore the sparks shooting from our clasped palms.

"You won't make it back to the guard's quarters, so you can sleep at mine."

He tries to protest, but I just ignore him. I drag him inside my unit and push him down on the sofa.

"Sleep," I command. He smiles dopily at me.

"You're cute when you're bossy."

My stomach does a flip, but I ignore it. I grab his legs and swing them onto the sofa. I unlace his boots and pull them off, putting them on the floor next to him.

"Why haven't you been sleeping?" I scold.

"Work," he says simply, his eyes are closed now. I start to stand to leave him to sleep when his hand grabs mine.

"Stay, please."

I hesitate before sitting back down.

"Missed you," he mutters, his voice is slurred. He must be really tired.

"I'm right here." He opens one eye a slit and then yanks me on top of him. I grunt when I hit his solid chest. I try to wiggle away but he spanks me. I stop in shock and stare at his smirking face.

"What the hell, Barrott?" I moan.

"Shh, I'm trying to sleep," he warns and then closes his eyes. I lay there, not daring to move. His breathing evens out and he's snoring before I can count to thirty. He must have been so tired. I know I can't stay here like this, the boys and Effie will be looking for me, not to mention if he wakes up like this, he will blame me and get uncomfortable.

I daren't move in case he wakes, so instead, I lay there for a while memorising the feel of his body beneath me. After a while, I sigh and make myself slip out of his arms. He grumbles and tries to grab me before turning over and going back to sleep. I look at his handsome face and then move some of his hair away from his eyes. I wish Effie was right about him liking me. With one last glance at my sleeping shadow, I slip out of my unit and head to the dining room, trying to ignore the feeling of his arms and body wrapped around me.

When I reach the dining room, I don't see anyone, so I sit at our table. I just sit and watch people for a while until a tray is dropped in front of me with a bang, making me jump. Auden grins and sits next to me with his own, Eldon sits on my other side with one. I grin and start eating, looking around for Effie. Auden tries to snatch my pudding and I slap his hand with my spoon and glare at him. He sticks his tongue out at me, and when he turns back around, I snatch his bread. He turns to me with narrowed eyed but grinning. I just shove the bread in my mouth, daring him to do something. He leans forward, a strange look in his eyes, when I hear Effie's voice. I frown and look around. She's trapped in the walkway between tables by Chrissy.

This girl just doesn't get it. I stand and stomp over to her. Chrissy's friends see me and back away. My face burns with my anger. The feeling of the brothers' story comes rushing back only, adding fuel to the fire. Chrissy puts her face right in Effie's and then laughs when she flinches.

"Stupid stuck up virgin," she mocks.

Oh, hell no. I walk faster, my eyes narrowed on her.

"Why don't you just do us a favour, and just disappear."

I don't bother stopping. I grab her arm and twist it behind her, slamming her down to the table in front of where she's standing. I look at Effie and wink. I see the tears in her eyes and my anger doubles. I breathe deeply, trying not to take this too far. I glare at Chrissy's friends.

"I ever see you going in on Effie or anyone else again, we are going to have a problem." They nod and scatter. I look back at Effie, ignoring Chrissy's wiggling beneath me. She is swearing and trying to move. Luckily, Barrott taught me some moves a while ago to protect myself.

"Hi, babe, why don't you go sit down." I turn back to Chrissy. People are standing watching us now, most are teenagers as the older people tend to have their dinner later to avoid all the classes coming out. I lean over her, pulling her arm up, making her swear louder.

"You are going to listen, and you are going to listen good this time. I ever see you near my family again, I will break this arm. You ever so much as look at her and I will make your life hell. I don't know what your problem is, but you leave Effie out of it. Understood?" She swears again, trying to get free. When she realises she can't, she stops and breathes heavily underneath me. I add a bit more pressure and she shouts.

"Okay. Fine, let me go!"

I give her arm another pull, just for good measure and then let her go and step back. I don't turn in case she tries to come after me. I wait. She straightens and whirls to me, hate in her eyes. Her face is red with a faint imprint from the table, I just wait. She obviously decides it's not worth the hassle and storms off. I turn back to Effie with a smile, she just shakes her head at me, but her tears have gone.

"Amazing, have I told you how hot it is when you get all riled up?" Cain's voice nearly makes me groan. I ignore him, grab Effie's arm and gently tug her to the table. Auden and Eldon are standing in the way, obviously trying to decide whether they needed to help. I just nod at them and they sit back down. Effie sits down, and I sit next to her. Cain leans over the table towards me.

"So, speed demon, when are you going to get all riled up for me again?" I grit my teeth and flip him off. He laughs, but flops down on the free chair at our table. This time I do groan.

"You okay Effie?" His usual attitude disappears as he offers her a friendly smile, she smiles back at him and nods. He turns back to me, his smirk in place.

"You coming to the party tonight?" My eyes are drawn to his lips and I quickly look back up, but it's too late. He caught me. He doesn't say anything, but his smirk grows.

"Maybe," I say, leaning back. His legs touch mine under the table and I don't bother moving away.

"Come on, speed demon, we have good times there." I can feel the brothers looking at me, but I just stare at Cain.

"I might, I've got dinner with Effie tonight; our usual weekly one." I hope sharing might make him go away.

"Sure thing Indy, I'll see you there though." Cain winks and then saunters off. I look back at Effie who is grinning now.

"Shut up," I tell her. I look at Auden and Eldon and see they are both looking at their food, their eyes tight and lips turned down in a frown. I shrug and then start eating.

"I haven't seen Barrott today?" Effie says while I'm chewing.

"Yeah, he's been working a lot. I found him nearly passed out in the hallway."

"Do you think it has anything to do with..." She looks around and lowers her voice "those Saviour people?" I sigh.

"Effie, they're just rumours." I smile gently at her. I know they aren't, but she doesn't need spooking.

"Yeah, we heard about them below," Auden adds. I nod. Who hasn't? Although, it would make sense they would target below more. More oppressed people, more fodder for their rebellion. The only reason I know it's true is I overheard Barrott one night. I asked him about it, he begrudgingly told me that it was true. There is a rebellion on-board the ship called The Saviours but apparently, they just want to cause trouble. He wouldn't tell me anymore, but I always make sure to keep my ears open. After all, what are they rebelling for?

"So, are you going to the party tonight?" Effie asks, eagerness in her voice. I groan, knowing what that means.

"If I have to." She wraps her arms around me.

"Thanks, Inds." She jumps up and heads off.

"Can we come?" Eldon asks, there's an odd note in his voice.

"Duh, I was expecting you to." They offer me big smiles, the first I've seen of them today, dimples and all.

"Meet me at my unit tonight after evening meal," I smile and head off as well.

I spend the afternoon in the simulator again, I daren't go back to my unit. By the time evening meal rolls around, I'm actually excited for the party. It's been a month or so since I've been to one. I head to Effie's unit. You're supposed to eat in the dining room, but every now and again you can take food to your unit. Me, Howard, and Effie have a private meal together every two weeks.

I don't bother buzzing, I just scan myself in. Their unit is smaller than mine, with only two bedrooms and a living room/dining room combo. I spot Howard dishing up food at the dining table and head his way with a genuine smile. He smiles when he spots me and puts the food down, holding out his arms. I let him hug me and step back before I can get sentimental. He looks at the table, then back at me.

"Thanks for the credits Indy." His voice is full of gratitude. I just nod, it's not like I need them. I won't use them when I get to Ayama as I'm coming back, so it means they get a better life. He never asks where I get them, I think he knows I will never say. He's not stupid though, he knows it's not legal. I sit down, and he serves me a plate.

"Where's Effie?" I ask. He nods upstairs and then I hear her skipping down.

"Sorry was picking my outfit out." I almost moan. Effie's a shy girl until she's had a drink. She doesn't often go to parties but when she does, she makes sure to get very drunk. I always end up dragging her home as she cries, apologising every two minutes.

The meal is nice. We keep the conversation light, but I see the strain around Howard's eyes. He's been working too much, I asked him why once. He said more and more things are breaking, something to do with accidents. What he didn't think I heard was his mumbled 'accidents my arse'

I make my excuses and head back to my unit to get changed. My heart falls when I see that Barrott has disappeared, I guess he has to work. I pull out some jeans and a shirt, then hesitate. I haven't dressed up in a while, and every girl likes to look nice sometimes. I dig out a skirt and slogan t-shirt and add my only pair of high heeled boots. I tell myself it's because I want to, not because of who's going. I even do something with my hair, adding serum to it to make it long loose waves, not its usual mess. I don't bother with makeup though. I look back in the mirror, admitting I look good. My legs are long and look good in the skirt, the shirt is loose enough over my breasts to not make them look ridiculous, and it shows off my slender waist.

The door buzzes, and I head down. Auden and Eldon stand on the other side and when I open it, they both look shocked. They are in matching jeans and tight t-shirts, both in different colours. It shows off their muscles. They run their eyes over me and can't seem to look away from my legs.

"Guys," I laugh. They both look up. Auden blushes, but smiles. Eldon just winks at me.

"Let's go get Effie and head to the party." They both nod, but I see them flicking their eyes in appreciation over me again.

TRANSMISSION LOG 00306
DATE: 2033
MISSION: 43, COLONY
SHIP: DAWNBREAKER
DESTINATION: AYAMA

>............ Accepted
>The attacks are getting more regular; engi-
neers and guards are pulling double shifts. We
have given the order to start raids, starting
on the lower levels and then working up. The
ship took some damage in the latest attack.
Please advise on how to proceed?

CHAPTER SIX

DAY 917

THE MUSIC IS BLARING, pulsing in time to my heartbeat. My smile is real, my worries and issues floating away with the beat. We grabbed Effie then made our way down to the party. It's being held in one of the end units, the kid's parents are some sort of higher up and never here. To the left, people are playing space pong. To the right, all the sofas have been moved and a dance floor has appeared. Sweaty bodies push against each other, grinding and dancing to the music. There's another room, I think it was once a game room, attached to the living room and I can see the crowd in there from here. I turn back to Auden, Eldon, and Effie where we are standing at the door surveying. The brothers look shocked, I guess they don't have these sorts of parties on the lowers.

"Come on guys, let's have some fun." I push through the crowd towards the game area. We stand against the wall, watching as the two people play; trying to get their balls in each other's cups. It's basically beer pong from Earth, but the cups move. So, space pong. Cain slides up next to me and offers me an unopened bottle. I grab it with a grateful smile.

"Thought you might come." He leans in and whispers in my ear, causing a shiver to go down my body. I ignore him, crack the lid and take a swig. Effie grabs it off me and takes a big drink and then coughs when the alcohol burns on its way down. She gives me the bottle back.

"I'm going to dance, I'll catch you guys in a bit."

I nod and watch her. She's wearing a floaty dress; it's cute, but it means she looks hotter than normal. I shake my head and worry on my bottom lip.

"She will be fine," Cain says casually. I roll my eyes, but honestly, his words settle me a bit.

"Want to play?" Cain nods at the table where the game is winding up. I turn to him with a smirk in place.

"Why? So I can kick your ass?" He laughs, the sound smooth and genuine.

"We'll play," Eldon adds, his voice hard.

"Doubles then." Cain winks at me. "I'll be on your team, speed demon."

"What, scared I'll beat you otherwise?"

His eyes lock on mine. "I'm not stupid, speed demon. Plus, it means I get to get all up close and personal. Did I mention how amazing you look in that skirt?" His eyes drop to my legs, and I roll mine. He might act like a perv sometimes, but as annoying as it is, he's actually a good guy. I turn to the brothers.

"So, us against you." I smile, and they flash their dimples.

"What's the winner get?" Auden asks and winks at me. I feel Cain step up behind me, the heat from his body warming my back. I only just stop myself from leaning back into him. I tilt my head in thought.

"How about this. You win, you pick. I win…" Cain coughs. "We win and you're on carrying home duty." Cain leans forward.

"I'll carry you home, darling."

I ignore him again. The brothers nod and then they step forward. I'm sandwiched between them and Cain. My heart speeds up.

"We win, and you have to dance with us." Eldon's eyes are warm and watch my reaction.

"Done." I slide out from between them, a little overwhelmed. I head to the now free table and start setting up the cups. Cain sits on the table facing me and watches. Eldon and Auden have grabbed a bottle from somewhere and are setting up their side. Some girl tries to get Cain's attention. but he ignores her.

"So, they your new toys?" Cain leans back and swings his legs. Honestly, it's annoying how good looking he is. He sits there looking like some sort of rock star and I'm supposed to remember how to speak.

"Why, you jealous?" I offer while filling the cups.

"Yep." I look up in shock. Me and Cain have always flirted, we play against each other and it's fun. I must look as shocked as I feel, because he laughs quietly.

"I've never hidden my interest, Indy. Any girl who can keep up with me-" He licks his lips and carries on, "Plus, I was trying to be a gentleman and give you space after your breakup." Anger spikes through me and I push it away at the reminder of my ex.

"You, a gentleman?" He frowns and I realise I've offended him. I stop and watch his face, maybe he's being serious? I consider it, it's true he never pushes me. He flirts hard but lets me have my space. Even that night when I drunkenly kissed him, he was the one to pull away. He told me if I wanted to do that while I was sober he would love it, but he wouldn't do anything while we were drunk.

"I am a gentleman, Indy. Just because I laugh and don't hide checking you out doesn't mean I'm not." He jumps up and stands at my side. He's rigid and I sigh - I have offended him.

"I know you can be, Cain. I guess I'm just not used to you being open," I say, looking at the brothers setting up.

"I'm always open, Indy, you're the one who's not. You run away from me, but it's okay. I know you will eventually come to me." He smiles at me and I smile back.

"Plus, it means I get to check you out in these amazing skirts as you bend over." I groan, at least the normal Cain is back.

"Ladies first," Auden says. I laugh, but take the ball. Stepping back, I throw it gently. It bounces off the side of the front cup and sinks into it. They look shocked, but pleased. I wink. Auden grabs the cup and downs it. Eldon throws the ball back to me and I pass it to Cain as a peace offering.

He throws but misses. It goes on like this for a while. I manage to sink three more and the brothers only two. I'm just lining up for my next shot when Effie stumbles to the table next to me. I stop and look at her, her eyes are glassy, and her face is flushed.

"There you are, Indy," her voice is high and slurring a little. I think this is a new record for how quickly she got drunk.

"You already drunk, Effs?" I lean my hip against the table and cross my arms.

"Just happy, babe. Mind if I watch?" She smiles brightly at me. Cain comes back with a chair and sits it next to the table, I didn't even notice him moving. She falls into it with a salute. I turn back to the table and sink my next shot. Effie claps and the brothers groan, they only have one left. Cain steps up behind me, grabbing the ball where it just bounced to our side. His arms bracket me, and he's pushed up against me.

"Er, Cain...?" I ask. He shushes me.

"I'm trying to concentrate here." An evil thought comes into my head. I lean back a little against him and he goes still. My lips twitch, but I just watch the brothers.

"Throw it then," I say with a laugh. He leans down to my ear.

"You are playing with fire, Indy." He leans back and throws. He misses completely, and I laugh and step away. I look at him and he grins at me. I like this side of Cain, I guess he's right; I never even gave him a chance. Effie starts chanting my name and a group is forming behind her watching us, mostly women, I note with annoyance.

Eldon takes the next throw and sinks it. He high fives Auden and I grab the cup. I down it and throw the ball back to them. Auden throws and sinks it again, Cain moans but takes the cup I offer him and drinks. Eldon throws again but misses when some girl plasters herself on his side. I grab the ball and my eyes narrow on her. Jealousy rises, and I don't even know why; it's not like we are dating. We're just friends. I concentrate on throwing, but I miss when she leans up and whispers in his ear. I grind my teeth, but look away. Auden grabs the ball and throws, he misses too. Cain grabs it and leans into me.

"If he goes with that skank over you, Indy, he's a fool." I look at him in surprise. He offers me a gentle smile.

"She's a nobody; you-" he breathes in, "you're amazing." He turns back to the table and lines up his next shot. I watch half-heartedly, my heart warming at his words. He manages to sink it; Eldon turns back with a groan and grabs the cup. Cain turns to me and picks me up at the waist. He spins me around and a laugh bubbles out of me. He puts me down and I high five him. I look back over the table and see another girl has joined the first, and they are both looking at the brothers. I watch as the other one puts her hand on Auden's chest. I let my narrowed eyes run over them; they're pretty. The one next to Eldon has long straight black hair and a cute face; her shorts are basically hot pants and her shirt leaves nothing to the imagination. The one with Auden has a stunning face and long blonde curly hair. Her skirt is plastered to her tanned skin and she's wearing a crop top. I grab a cup and take a swig.

I don't know why it's bothering me so much. They are good looking, of course girls will notice. I turn away and meet Effie's eyes. She was glaring at the girls. I grab her hand and pull her up.

"Let's dance, babe." She throws the girls one more glare but follows me. I drain the cup and put it on a table as we pass.

I drag her to the dance floor and we start gyrating to the beat. My eyes run back over the crowd and my heart drops when I don't see the brothers or the girls anywhere. Cain is leaning against the table we were just playing at, a cup in his hand. His gaze is locked on me. Some girl is talking at his side, but he doesn't seem to be listening. I turn back, avoiding the intensity in his gaze. Me and

Effie dance for a couple of songs, but I'm done with drinking. The idea of the brothers off with the two girls has made my stomach churn. Effie stops and wipes her sweaty forehead. She grabs my hand and pulls me from the crowd towards Cain.

"God, that whiskey has made me feel weird," she moans. I look her over.

"You okay?" she nods and pulls me along. Cain smirks when we reach him.

"Where are Auden and Eldon?" Effie asks, confused. He shrugs but looks at me. I look away, trying to show it doesn't bother me. Effie groans and stumbles into me. I look at her with a frown. She grabs her head and leans against me.

"Babe, I don't feel well. Can we go?" Her voice is quiet, and her face is pale. I grab her hand.

"Sure, let's get out of here. I'll walk you back." She offers me a strained smile. Cain puts his drink down.

"I'll come." I raise my eyebrow in shock. He just smiles and leads us from the party. I look around one last time but don't spot the brothers. I try to not let it bother me. We walk in silence back to Effie's. Halfway there, she stops and bends over dry heaving. I rub her back. Eventually, she stops and looks at me with tears in her eyes.

"Sorry, Indy." Her voice is slurred, and the last word ends on a burp.

"It's okay, babe. Let's get you home, okay?" She nods, and I try and pull her along, but she stumbles. Cain stops and turns to her.

"Can I carry you, Effie?" She looks at me, but I don't protest. She nods. She must be really feeling bad. He scoops her up gently and follows me back to her unit. When we get there, I direct him to her bedroom and stand aside as he gently puts her on her bed. I grab her shoes and pull them off and cover her up. She groans and burrows into her bed. I turn back to Cain.

"Thank you," I whisper. He smiles gently and then strokes my cheek.

"Any time, speed demon," he whispers, just as soft. Effie makes another noise and I flick my head to the door. He nods and leaves. I lean over her.

"Night, Effie." I kiss her sweaty forehead.

"Love you," she mumbles.

"Love you, too." I head out after Cain and find him leaning on the wall outside her unit.

"You going home?" he asks, shoving his hands in his jean pockets. I hesitate, I really don't want to go home. The brothers were supposed to be staying tonight and I know I'll just sit there thinking about what they are doing. Cain watches my internal dilemma and then straightens.

"Do you trust me?" his voice is soft and hesitant. I take a breath and let it out. Do I? I look him over.

"Yes," I offer truthfully. The smile he flashes me is so opposite his usual smirk, it throws me. It makes him look handsome and so dangerous to my heart. He grabs my hand and tugs me along.

"Where are we going?" I ask when he doesn't say anything. He looks at me and winks.

"You'll see." I let him lead me along, my heart beating faster at the feel of his hand in mine and the fact that it's now just us two. He leads me through some upper levels doors I've never been in before. He stops before a door and scans his hand. When it flashes green, he smiles at me and pulls me through.

The room is dark, and I hesitate.

"I swear if you think-" I start. He laughs, and just pulls me along. I grumble but follow. I gasp when I see where we are. Stumbling to a stop, I stare in awe. It's stupid, I know we are in space, but it's easy to forget. There's not a lot of windows anywhere and it doesn't feel like you are on a ship, but the window in front of me reminds me. It's spread halfway up the ceiling and down to the floor; offering an undisturbed view of the stars and the sky. I turn back to him in wonder.

"How?" He offers me that smile again.

"I've got to have some secrets, Indy." He pulls me after him and then drops to the floor. He lays there, looking up at the stars, hands behind his head. I lay next to him and stare at the stars in silence. I can hear his breathing, but the silence doesn't feel uncomfortable. I loosen up a bit and really look at the sky. It's amazing.

"I love coming here. There's no one watching you, expecting anything. You can just be you." His voice is soft, and I turn my head to see he's still looking at the stars, so I do the same.

"I know what you mean."

"I know." His voice is still soft.

"How did you know this was here?" I'm really curious. He doesn't answer for a while and I look at him. He is nibbling on his lip, looking hesitant.

"You know I'm an upper, right?" He eventually asks. I frown. I didn't. I guess I should have, but I never really thought about it.

"No." He looks at me and smiles a little shyly. It's so opposite from the usual Cain.

"Well, I am. I'm not close to any of my family. They don't have time for me. I spend loads of time exploring, and one day I found this. It's like my own personal retreat." I look back at the stars, thinking his words through. If he's an upper, I can imagine the looks he was talking about.

"So, an upper slumming it and racing. How scandalous," I joke. He cups my cheek and turns me to face him.

"I'm not slumming it, Indy. My parents might be uppers, but I'm not. They earned that; I haven't. I don't care about titles and labels, I just want to be happy. I never got a choice to come into space, but I plan on making the most of it." The honesty in his words draws mine. He strokes my cheekbone and watches me.

"I know what you mean. My parents are- were- brilliant. I'm not. They got this opportunity and didn't think to ask me. I had to leave everything; and I love them, I do. I always will, but I just wish they had asked."

He nods, "Me too."

I smile at him and he returns it.

"You're not so bad for an upper," I joke.

"You're not so bad yourself." His voice is serious, but I ignore the undertone. I turn back to the stars and so does he.

"I guess I forget sometimes where we are." He grabs my hand and twines his with it. I don't protest, it feels good. I accept the comfort in his offering and, for the first time in a long time, I'm just in the moment, laying myself bare.

"It's easy to. So, the great Indy, what are you going to do when we get there?" His voice is teasing. I hesitate, but I know Cain. He won't judge me, it's just not in him.

"Nothing. I plan on going back as part of the flight crew." His hand stills for a moment before playing with my fingers again.

"Too bad, we could have caused some havoc." I laugh, just like he knew I would.

"I get why though, Indy." His voice is quiet, and the room is filled with sadness. I push it away.

"So, what will Cain, the great upper, do?" I ask cutting through the somber mood that my parent's memory causes.

"Honestly, I don't know. I might be in my element here. I'm a good racer, girls flock to me, everyone loves me. But on the ground, I don't know." He's not bragging, he's just telling the truth.

"Whatever it is, you will be amazing at it." I see him turn to me, but don't look.

"You think so?" His voice is shy and filled with uncertainty.

"Yep, it's not in you to not give something your all. You don't value your skills enough. You didn't get on this ship just because of your parents." My words ring true. "They might be the reason why we are considered but we all have to pass tests and be useful." I hear his breath shakily leaving him.

"Thank you, Indy."

"Thank you for bringing me here." I see him smile out of the corner of my eye.

"Whenever you need to escape, you let me know." His voice is back to his usual confident self, but now I know what's underneath. I will never be able to look at him the same and that makes my heart speed up.

We spend a couple of hours watching the stars and talking. When he walks me back to my unit, there's something different between us that scares and intrigues me. He doesn't even try anything when we get to my door, just smiles at me and leaves.

I scan my hand, lost in my thoughts, and stop at the sight that greets me. Barrott is pacing in my living room and the brothers are sitting on my sofa looking tense. Barrott spots me first and stomps over to me.

"Where the hell have you been? I get to your door to find these two idiots have lost you at a party? Do you know how worried I was? Anything could have happened to you, I even looked through the cameras." I let him rant, seeing the fear in his eyes.

"I'm fine. I had to take Effie home; she wasn't feeling well." His eyes narrow to slits.

"And then where did you go?" He growls, crossing his arms over his chest.

"For a walk." I don't want to tell him about me and Cain, it feels like a secret; something only we need to know. I walk around him, ignoring the waves of anger rolling off him and then collapse in the sofa opposite the brothers. They frown at me.

"Why didn't you get us?" Auden asks. He looks sad.

"You were busy," I shrug. They both watch me, I can't read their expression.

"Don't do that again, Indy," Barrott shouts. I stand up, suddenly angry.

"I am an adult, Barrott. If I want to go to a party and then go for a walk, I will." I shout back. "Stop treating me like a kid!" I fume. He stares at me, his shoulders tight and his face hard.

"Maybe I would if you stopped acting like one. Do you know what it's like worrying about you twenty-four seven because I never know what stupid thing you are going to do next? It's like a burden on my chest." I step back like he slapped me. You know that feeling when your whole body aches and your chest feels constricted? Yeah, it sucks. It only makes me angrier though - in a simple sentence he can hurt me so much.

"I am not your burden. You owe me nothing, just because you were there the day my parents died. I'm not your family, I'm not even your friend." My voice is venomous and covers my heart breaking at his words. He stops and stares me at me. I think he just realised what he said, but it's too late.

"Indy, I didn't mean-" His radio crackles and we both stare at it.

"Go, I don't want you here and stop following me." I stomp off to my room, needing to get away before he sees my tears. I told Effie he thought of me like some kid sister and his harsh words just confirmed it. Why did she have to get my hopes up? I get into my bed and lay on my side. Today started so well and now it's gone to shit. I eventually hear the door to my unit closing and my heart goes with it. I hear footsteps, but I ignore them, my back to the door. The bed dips as one of the brothers curls up behind me. Auden walks around the bed and lays in front of me, his back facing me. I'm stiff in Eldon's arms, my thoughts still on where they were earlier. Auden slides back, as close to me as he can get. He grabs my arm, wrapping it around him. His hands holds my other hand against his chest. Eldon wraps his arm around me tighter.

"We weren't busy," he starts. I stay quiet.

"We got rid of those annoying girls and went to get another drink while you were dancing. The queue was huge, and when we got back, you were gone. We searched for you when we realised you weren't there. We left straight away and came here." Eldon's voice is soft and heals my hurting heart a bit. The hole that Barrott left jagged and painful.

"You didn't have to, you could have gone with those girls," I

65

mutter. Auden's body shakes with silent laughs and Eldon laughs out loud. I tense again, he snuggles up behind me closer.

"It's cute when you're jealous, good looking, but let me make something clear. We didn't want those girls, we don't want any but the one in our arms right now." My heart speeds up and all my jealousy and anger disappears.

"Really?" My voice is soft and shy.

"Really," Auden says.

"We knew it the first day we saw you. You're not like other girls and we love it." Eldon says against the back of my head.

"But how does this-" I start, questions tumbling from my lips.

"Shh, let's leave everything for another day. All you need to know is: we want you, Indy." I nod and smile, my heart aches a bit less. I lay between them and drift off to sleep, but my heart clenches at the thought of Barrott, and pain spikes through me. My eyes fill as I remember his words. I hide it in Auden's back. My body is between the brothers, but my heart is out there with my surly shadow- not mine anymore.

Even though he said I'm a burden, I can't imagine my life without him. I wonder if he will listen to me and leave me alone. I don't know which I want. Either way will hurt. To have him always with me, but unable to touch him, is torture. But not having him in my life? I can't imagine it.

***

TRANSMISSION LOG 00307
DATE: 2033
MISSION: 43, COLONY
SHIP: DAWNBREAKER
DESTINATION: AYAMA

>.............. Accepted
>There was a large attack last night. One of
the loading bays sustained serious damage. The
rebels have claimed responsibility. They have
warned us it will only get worse until we tell
everyone. Please advise on how to proceed?

CHAPTER SEVEN

DAY 918

I WAKE up before the boys, still warm and cocooned in their arms. Grudgingly, I slide out of the bottom of the bed without waking them. I freeze when Eldon grumbles in his sleep and cuddles to his brother's back, throwing his arm over his middle. Covering my mouth with my hand, I hold on to the giggle at how adorable it is. It's times like this that make me wish we still had ways to capture and save imagery, cameras I think they were called. It's a sad thing that they were deemed useless and a waste of resources.

I shower and make my way downstairs. As I wander into the kitchen area, I notice the comms unit blinking with a message waiting for me. Clicking the symbol, I access the message.

Tonight.

Excitement runs through me. It's exactly what I need after what happened with Barrott last night. I can lose myself and let the hurt out. Plus, I get to see Cain again. Lost in my thoughts, I jump when arms wrap around my waist from behind. One of the brothers buries his head in my hair and just breathes me in. Eldon appears in front of me with a smile, so it must be Auden. His smile turns gentle when he looks at me in his brother's arms.

"Come on, good looking. Time for breakfast." he says before brushing a gentle kiss on my forehead. Auden mumbles again, tightening his hold on me. Laughing, I try and step away. I don't know what sort of mess I would be in if they weren't here right

68

now. Probably be replaying every little detail from mine and Barrott's fight. Yet, I find myself enjoying this time I have with them even if a storm hovers over me; threatening to sink me back into its depths at the slightest provocation.

Auden clings onto me like a monkey, bringing me back to the here and now.

"No. My Indy," he says louder before burying his face into my neck. I laugh again, Eldon rolls his eyes, but his smile widens.

"If you let Indy go, we can get food," he offers, I feel Auden physically hesitate.

"I'll even give you my bread," I offer. He grins against my neck.

"Promise?"

"Promise," I say sweetly. He kisses my neck, sending a shiver through me and making my stomach flop. He lets me go and rushes to the door, looking back at us like an eager kid.

"Come on then," he whines as he bounces on his toes. Still laughing, I follow him, a grinning Eldon not far behind.

It turns out to be just me and the brothers at breakfast. Effie sends me a message as I'm leaving for training saying she overslept and is hung over and Cain is probably wandering somewhere. I don't even want to think about Barrott. I turn to the guys just before I leave.

"Oh, I forgot to tell you, there's a race tonight if you still want to go?" Both of their faces brighten and then they nod vigorously in sync.

"I'll meet you later on then," I say around a wide smile, they both swoop in and drop kisses on either cheek before disappearing, muttering excitedly to each other. My mood is bright but instantly sours when I get to the loading bay. There's tape across the door and guards milling around everywhere. Some are armed and watching everyone come and go suspiciously. My happy bubble that the brothers created bursts, the storm swooping in. I really need to distract myself from the fight and flight training is my usual way, but it looks like that won't be happening. Frowning,

I spot the other trainees standing against the wall. I slowly walk over to them.

"What happened?" I ask all of them. A middle-aged man named Gus spares me a look.

"Training is cancelled, apparently there was a pipe explosion." It takes me a while to figure out what he said because of his strong accent, but when I do, I only frown harder, studying the bay door.

Why would the guards need to be here for a pipe explosion? Plus, I don't think any of the pipes in there would explode, after all, safety mechanisms were put in place for such a thing. My dad even told me so as he watched them be installed. Questions turn over and over in my head and are only stopped when one of our trainers stops and clears his throat before us.

"Sorry for the delay. We were talking over the plan. Training is cancelled for the rest of the week. We will let you know when it's back on." He is smiling at us, but it seems forced and something in his eyes has mine narrowing in suspicion. Why is he sweating? He seems nervous.

"Will we get to make up the time? And what about the test?" One of the others asks.

"We will run the test next week and you will all get extra time." His smile is so forced, I feel it might crack.

"What happened?" I ask loudly. He turns to me, his smile fading when he realises who asked. He glances back hesitantly before swallowing and looking back at me.

"Pipe explosion," he offers, sounding unsure.

"In the loading bay? Where the pipes are all locked behind steel walls and are checked every week?" I ask sarcastically, my dad's knowledge easily coming to me. He shuffles from side to side not looking at me.

"I don't know the details, but I can assure you we are getting it fixed and making sure it doesn't happen again." He smiles again and turns on his heel, marching away. The others talk between themselves and wander off, but I stay near the wall; watching. The guards are carrying weapons and scanning everything, not just the people. I see the door slide open for the instructor and catch a look inside. That was no pipe explosion.

I frown, but wander away, knowing the guards will usher me away soon. My curiosity is getting the better of me and I really want to ask Barrott, but I don't want to with our fight still fresh in my mind. Taking a deep breath, I try to come up with a plan.

I mean, it has nothing to do with me. Plus, the crew will deal with it, but even my own thoughts do nothing to dampen my curiosity. I shake my thoughts away and instead head to the lagoon to swim laps, hoping that will improve my mood. After an hour or so of swimming, an idea pops into my head. Racing to the shore, I dry off and head over to the medical wing to see Effie. She's frazzled, running around manically when I walk in. She glances at me before holding her hand up in a wait sign. Nodding, I rock back and forth on my heels.

The walls in here are painted white and grey and hover beds are placed around the large room, with holo screens ready to turn opaque when needed. Unlike the old Earth hospital, you find on those movies Effie loves so much, there's no wires and machinery anywhere. Instead, each doctor has a palm analyzer and scanner. Injections are done with nanobots and surgeries are practically a thing of the past with all our technology. I watch as Effie approaches a man clutching half of his face, screaming so much he is almost jackknifing off the bed. Blood and puss are everywhere, and it looks like a nasty burn. She waves her metal scanner over him and nods to herself at the results. She quickly programmes the bots and presses the scanner into his neck. He instantly relaxes, his eyes dilating with the pain meds and the nanobots work to reconstruct his face. Turning away, she presses the holoscreen, which turns grey. She stops and talks to another doctor before offering him a reassuring smile. Turning, she frowns at me, jerking her head in the direction of the corner of the room. Away from prying eyes. I follow after her, waiting until she turns. She runs her eyes over me worriedly, checking for injuries.

"Is everything okay?" she asks. I can understand why, I never come here, after all. It reminds me too much of that day. I pull myself out of my memories, my mind occupied with thoughts of the 'explosion.'

"Sure. Just wondered if your dad was at work today?" She looks at me strangely.

"Erm yeah, down on D-Deck." Someone shouts her name and she looks at them and waves.

"I gotta go." She looks back at me. "You sure you're okay?" She asks, concern lacing her words. I force a smile.

"Yep, fine." Nodding, she turns away.

"Oh Effie, have you heard anything about a pipe explosion?" She looks around and then steps closer to me again.

"Yeah, why?"

I shrug. "Just curious." She looks at me in that weird way, but answers.

"Some guys got brought in this morning from the loading bay." Looking around again, she lowers her voice. "But the wounds didn't make sense for a simple pipe explosion."

I tilt my head. "How so?" She fidgets with her scanners, pursing her lips.

"It's hard to explain, they looked like they had been in a fire. I thought the pipes in there automatically freeze when damaged which would mean shrapnel cuts, at worst but..." Someone shouts her name again and she gives me one last look. She's right. If the pipes in the bay had exploded, there wouldn't be fire; it's a safety precaution. And to only be limited to the bay?

"Don't say anything 'kay? See you later." She waves and runs off, her mind already on her next patient.

I was going to ask Howard about it. I want to see if I'm right about the pipes, but when I get to D-Deck, he's not there. With a defeated sigh, I head back to my unit. Something weird is going on. First, Barrott is working longer and longer shifts and complaining. Then, Howard mentioned the accidents aren't accidents, and now they are covering something up in the loading bay? Something is bugging me, but I don't know what. I know most people would be happy to have the week off and accept the excuses, but if there's something going on, I need to know so I can protect Effie and Howard. It doesn't help that I have a brain that won't let me forget and I have an obsession with trying to solve puzzles. I blame my mum for that. Thinking about her has her last words echoing in my head, making me suck in a deep breath.

Look for the truth.

What truth, and how did she know something would happen? Logically, she must have, it's too specific a thing to warn me of. Frowning, I rub my head. There were other people there that day. Maybe she didn't want to give anything away so tried to warn me without being specific. But if so, what was she telling me to look for? Freezing, I think back over the accident that killed them. It was a fire too... in a sealed, controlled lab? I try to remember the specifics, but I wasn't paying much attention back then. Surely it can't all be connected. Frustrated, I braid my hair trying to think through everything. In the end, all I have is more questions.

I spend the rest of the day trying to relax, in vain. Ideas and theories run through my head and it's only when the door buzzes that I let myself shake them away. The brothers are waiting on the other side, excitement etched on their faces for the race. It fuels my own, letting me escape my own thoughts. Hopefully, I can let go for a while.

We head down to the races, sneaking through the airlock to the lower area. When we reach the edge of the crowd, they both look overwhelmed. I guess they didn't realise how big it was. Dragging my eyes over the hundreds of people and the race track, I can understand why. The first time I saw it, I knew I had to be a part of it. Not to mention, when I saw the first race, my heart was beating in time to the stomping, my hands clutching the railing like a wheel as I imagined I was the one in the speeder. I approached Lee that night and told him I would do whatever it takes to be in the next race. The rest, as they say, is history. He gave me a chance and when he saw I was a natural, he guaranteed my spot at each and every race. Grinning at the brothers, the crowd's excitement mounting my I own, I drag them to two seats up front and push them down. I can almost taste the adrenaline, making me want to get started all that much quicker. I just wish Effie didn't have to work because of the explosion.

"Okay, stay here. I'll be back when I'm done."

They look at me and I laugh at their expressions.

"Be good," I kiss them both on their cheeks like they do to me. As I'm pulling back, Eldon grabs my arm.

"Wait, this is safe right?" he asks, concern flashing in his eyes. I laugh again.

"Nope, not even a little." I wave while turning. Vaulting over the railing, I wander over to the race track. Smiling, I make my way to the speeders which are already lined up ready for the drivers. Lee is standing over to the side talking to Cain, he turns and smiles when he sees me. I offer him a smile, but head over to my speeder. I can't afford to be distracted. I leave the door open and slide into the seat, flipping the on switch. I watch as the four holo screens light up. There are only two seats in mine, the three from the back were removed to make me faster. The screens cover the right-hand side and down to the control panel next to the driver's seat, waiting for me.

"Driver recognition," the automated voice asks.

"Indy Stewart."

"*Welcome back, Indy.*" The computer chimes, alerting me that my controls have been set up.

"I was hoping you'd be here."

I look up and smile. Cain is leaning against the door, his arms braced on the roof.

"Worried you might win if I wasn't?" I wink. He smirks, his cocky attitude back in full force.

"Nah, there's no competition without you."

I lean back in my bucket seat.

"See you brought them." He nods over at the brothers, who are watching us with a weird expression on their faces. Nodding, I look back at him, trying to ignore the muscles which are pushing against his shirt.

"Misunderstanding," I offer. He nods, but something flickers across his face too fast for me to catch it.

"Want to make this more interesting?" He wiggles his eyebrows, making me grin.

"Sure. What do I get when I win?" He laughs and leans into the cab.

"I win, and you come with me tonight to our spot. You win, and I'll bow down to you in front of everyone."

I tap my chin, pretending to ponder his bet.

"Hmm... a night with the ever annoying or a smackdown in front of everyone," my grin stretches across my face. "Deal."

The speaker sounds overhead, as Lee welcomes everyone. Cain leans in further, just inches separating us. My traitorous heart speeds up for a reason other than the racing, and my eyes drop to his plump lips.

"Now I have a reason to win. See you at the finish line." He winks and saunters to his speeder. Blowing out a disappointed breath, I lean out to close my door and get ready. Blocking out the crowd, I focus on the countdown appearing on the screen and with each glowing number my excitement builds...

10

9

8

7

6

5

The numbers flash on the console before me and the crowd goes wild chanting mine and Cain's name.

4

3

2

I grip the wheel and rev the engine, my grin turning crazy.

1

GO

I shoot out of the line, Cain not far behind me. I accelerate around the first corner, flicking my eyes back to see a speeder turning over and crashing. A new driver, I think with a snort. The S bend ahead slows me a little, but not much. I could probably run this track in my sleep. On the straight stretch, Cain pulls even with me and blows me a kiss, before pulling ahead. Laughing, I speed up. We pull even again, but he cuts the next corner tight, forcing me to pull behind him. I ignore all the other drivers, the race just between me and him. The ramp to the next level is ahead and I speed up yet again, the adrenaline coursing through my body. We both reach it side by side and the small jump down to the second level is smooth. I pull ahead, drifting around the corner. I turn bend after bend, blocking him and laughing crazily. The steep ramp back down comes up and I slow a little so I don't go flying. We rush over the starting line and around the first bend.

Shit.

The speeder from earlier hasn't moved and is blocking the middle of the track with room for only one speeder to go around it at a time. Cain and I are neck and neck, not wanting to give ground to the other. It's like playing chicken. I speed up, heading straight for the crashed speeder. The crowd is screaming; thinking we are both going to hit it. At the last minute, Cain pulls back, letting me swerve around it, him closely following.

We complete three more laps, trading first place more than once. In the last bit of the fourth lap, when I should slow for the ramp down, I speed up. I go flying over it, a moment of weightlessness hitting me as I come out of my seat. I tighten my hands, ready for the rough landing while I'm in the air. I crash back down on the course, having to grip the wheel to stay straight. Laughing, I drift through the finish line, spinning the speeder in a circle before stopping. My hands still clutching the wheel, my body tightly wired. A whoop bursts out of me as I let go and try to get my body under control. Getting out of the speeder, I watch as Cain pulls up next to me. I wait as he slides out, his gaze locked on me like no one else exists. I know the screen above must be focused on us, the crowd watching as he walks towards me. He's smiling that soft smile from the other night and suddenly I don't care anymore. If he kissed me right now, I would kiss him back. Even knowing the brothers are watching, even knowing my heart is pulling me in all directions.

"Crazy stunt, babe."

I wink at him and lean back on the speeder, trying to control myself. Seriously, how can I be attracted to so many people at once, and why does my stupid head not seem to care about that?

"Guess that means I win," I say smugly. He groans but steps up in front of me. He bends and bows to me at the waist in front of everyone with a flourish. The crowd goes crazy as I laugh. The great and popular upper bowing to a middle? Unheard of. He straightens and winks at me, showing me he's not bothered. He steps closer again and I blame my adrenaline for making my heart beat faster. Barely any room separates us now. I find myself holding my breath to see what he will do.

"I am sad that I don't get my prize though," he says slowly and pouts at me.

"Who says I won't go with you still?" I tilt my head. It's like the world stops, this moment so important. The crowd, the pressure of everything, fades away.

"Will you?" he asks unsure, he seems to have forgotten about everyone else too. His mask slipping to show me his other side.

"Yes," I say softly, my attitude disappearing as the word slips out. That brilliant smile graces his face, making me swallow hard as he watches me with tender eyes. Straightening before I do something crazy like jump him, I slip past, breaking the moment.

"I'll see you tonight," I offer before heading over to Lee.

"Good race, Indy!"

I nod at him, my head still muddled from the adrenaline and Cain.

"Usual?" he asks

"Yeah, thanks Lee." My eyes lose focus as I try to think of a way to sort out my stupid attraction to them all once and for all.

"Why do you give them all your winnings?" Lee asks as he types on his tablet, disrupting my thoughts. Blinking, I watch him before answering.

"They are my family, it means they can have a better life on the ground. Bigger house, more food, even take the time off to enjoy Ayama..," I trail off as he raises his head, his eyes watching me seriously.

"And you don't need that?"

"Why would I? I don't plan on staying." Ignoring his surprised look, I spin and head over to the brothers. They sweep me up in a hug, making me giggle.

"So, what did you guys think?" I ask when they put me down.

"That was crazy! I've never been so scared and excited at the same time," Auden gushes. I look at Eldon.

"You were great, good looking, I was a little scared though." I offer him a smile in reassurance.

I look around the crowd, my eyes flitting from person to person. They land on a man and a woman. I don't know what makes me look at them. With a frown, I realise they are watching me and not the other competitors or Lee. The man is tall with a bald head and a face you would easily forget, the woman at his side has long black hair. They seem familiar, but I don't know why. The woman offers me a smile before they both disappear into the crowd.

Turning back to the guys to ask if they noticed them, I swallow the question when I notice they are busy smiling at me. I offer them a tentative one back and forget the weird woman and man.

"Let's get out of here." They both nod, each grabbing a hand. I look back at Cain to see him watching us, a strange expression on his face... Dare I say it looks thoughtful?

We spend the rest of the evening at the lagoon, racing and playing. My bad mood once again disappearing with their banter. Each time they touch me, it seems to linger, and more than once I catch them watching me when they think I'm not looking.

When it comes to going back to the unit, I'm surprised when they tell me they are going to stop at their own. I've gotten used to them staying at mine, and once I step through the door, I notice how quiet it is now. All the memories and belongings I was holding onto to remember my parents, only seem to add to the ache. This place should be filled with joy and happiness, instead, it's like a museum - or a tomb. With determined steps, I start to tidy up all the stuff they left all over the place the morning of the accident.

For once, the sadness is manageable and instead, I can look at the memories that the objects hold without breaking down. I put them all gently in a box for storage, my fingers lingering over their notes. I remember a time I could barely look at their handwriting without breaking down, now each day seems to get easier. I will never forget them, but it doesn't hurt as much to remember them now. I don't just think of their deaths, but their lives too. Remembering everything we did together, all the birthdays and days spent as a family. I think the pain will always be there, but maybe not as strong, until one day, all that's left is the good, not the bad. It brings down a wall in me, one I use to push people away. The one that tells me that everyone leaves. Until I'm left feeling more human, less of the girl who used every excuse to find a way to forget, to keep busy. Instead, I can be in my own company without going mad. I can sit and think through my feelings without pain or anger. I think Auden, Eldon and even Barrott and Cain are a large part of why.

I'm just clearing away the table when the buzzer goes, looking through the camera I grin when I see Cain. Opening the door, I casually lean against it. His hands are shoved in his jeans pockets and his smile is shy. This is my favourite version of Cain.

"You still want to go?" His words almost seem to burst out of him and I notice with mirth his cheeks tint.

"I said I would, didn't I?" I offer, not moving. His shoulders drop, I didn't even notice how tense they were before. His smile grows into his usual cocky smirk.

"Hurry up then, speed demon."

I roll my eyes, but step out and shut the door behind me. He grabs my hand, twining his fingers with mine. I notice his palms are sweaty. Glancing at him out of the corner of my eye, I wonder if he is nervous? Why does this feel so different than any other relationship I've been in? Not that we are in a relationship, but with all the others it was like I was going through the motions. Doing what was expected. It doesn't mean I didn't care, but this just feels more. More right, more exciting, like it's meant to be. Every little word making my heart flutter like a trapped bird and every touch feel like the first time all over again. But how can one person feel like that for four people? More to the point, how will they react when they find out? Pushing my fears and doubts aside, I let myself be in this moment. If I'm going to mess it up by admitting I have feelings for someone else, I want to remember this without them clouding my every move.

We are talking and joking as we walk, sharing smiles and giggles like teenagers on their first date. Well, I guess we sort of are. This past year has made me feel older than just my eighteen years, but it's nice to feel young for once. I catch movement out of the corner of my eye, making me glance to see the back of a retreating guard. I eye the walk and the back, is that Barrott? I watch as he turns the corner, his shoulders slumped and his head low. Was he coming to see me? I'm pulled from my questions when Cain tugs on my hand.

I almost groan when Chrissy steps out of a corner into us, her usual sidekicks behind her. She glances from Cain to me and then down to our joined hands. Her smile turns into a frown, but she quickly wipes it away, her painted lips twisting into something more friendly. It does nothing to detract from the calculative gleam in her eye. Ignoring me completely, she steps into Cain and leans her hand on his chest, fluttering her eyes at him.

"Hi, Cain," she purrs. Really? He looks uncomfortable, but offers her his usual smirk. I swear, if he starts flirting with her in front of me... I try to tug my hand back, but he doesn't let me.

"You were really good tonight, maybe you could take me racing with you sometime?" Her voice is low, and I'm sure it's supposed to be seductive. To me, she sounds like she's constipated. She starts stroking his chest and I've just decided I've had enough when he steps back and pulls me in front of him, my back to his chest. He wraps his arm around my waist and uses me as a shield from her. I have to choke down my laugh.

"Save me, speed demon," he whispers to me. Feeling more secure now that I know he's not going to flirt with her, I lean back against him, getting comfy. Her face is like a thunderstorm and she's glaring daggers at me. The next second, she's all smiles again. It's creepy.

I pretend to inspect my nails, ignoring her.

"Why don't you run along Indy, me and Cainy have some things we need to discuss." She licks her lips at him and I nearly vomit. Cainy? I have to bite my tongue to stop the laugh from coming out. I feel him shudder in horror behind me.

"That's alright, thanks..." He trails off, does he really not know her name? He does sound confused. She frowns again.

"Chrissy," I supply helpfully. She glares at me again before smiling at Cain.

"Right, sorry Chrissy, but me and speed demon here are busy.

Why don't you ask one of the other racers?" His voice is cheerful. In this moment I fall a little bit in love with him. I'm betting he knows her name but is trying to make me feel better. All my insecurity and anxiety at seeing her vanishes. I offer her a genuine smile for the first time ever, too full of happiness to care. She stamps her foot, I shit you not. Stamps her foot like a child. She adds a pout as well and the laughter I've been trying to hold in tumbles out. Remind me to never pout if that's what I look like, seriously. She looks like a duck or like she just sucked on a lemon.

"Shut the fuck up, Indy," she hisses. "You're such a slut, first Liam and now Cain? Or is it those brothers who follow you around like lost puppies?" My laughter dries up at the arse badger's name.

"Chris are you…" Say the jizz cock's name once and he appears. Ugh, I'm so telling Effie my theory about using insults to name him, sort of like how they never say Voldemort in those movies, was a good idea. He rounds the corner and looks between us all, wincing when he notices me in Cain's arms. He ignores Chrissy and stares at me. I look him over, it looks like he's lost weight. He's still handsome, with those baby blues I loved so much and his styled brown hair. He doesn't compare to the brothers or Cain though. He's got muscle and is quite tall, but now when I look at him, I don't feel anything.

"Indy." His voice is full of awe. I haven't seen him since that night. I avoided him like the plague until I didn't care anymore and then I just never noticed if he was around. I never loved him, maybe if we had been together long enough, I could have. He is smart, funny and good looking, so it's not a stretch. I definitely felt something for him but compared to my feelings for Cain, and even the brothers, it's like the wind blowing versus a tornado. I just nod at him. Chrissy sidles up to him, wrapping herself around him. He doesn't even glance at her.

"Hi, babe," she purrs and leans up to kiss his cheek. He blinks and looks at her as if he just realised she was there. He looks uncomfortable in her arms, making me feel a little sorry for him.

Cain tugs me and we turn to leave, leaving the happy couple to it.

"Indy, wait!"

I stop with a groan. Cain looks at me with a raised eyebrow, asking me what I want to do. Shaking my head at my own foolishness, I turn and look at them.

"What's up?" I ask as casually as I can.

He steps away from Chrissy and the look she gives him is murderous. "Can we talk?"

My eyes round with shock. "About what?" Cain leans at my back, offering his support.

"Us?" He looks from Cain to me.

"There is no us?" I ask, genuinely confused.

"Give me a chance to explain, darling," I freeze at the endearment. "You cut me out and never let me..." He trails off, probably at the anger on my face.

"Look, douche canoe. I don't know what you think you will gain by talking to me. We were over ages ago. The fact is, I haven't thought about you, I don't want you, and I certainly don't care about your excuses. I've moved on, why can't you?" He looks like I've just slapped him.

"We were good together..." He starts hesitantly before I step closer, all my hurt from that time rushing back. I need him to understand, even if it is in the past.

"We were. until you couldn't handle it and ran to the closest girl. You freaked at having to be in a relationship when it wasn't just me supporting you. Because, let's face it, that's all it was between us. We were bored, and when I actually needed you to act like a boyfriend, you didn't." Tears fill his eyes and all I feel is pity. I take a breath, letting my anger disappear. The truth is he did me a favour that day. I would have probably stayed with him instead of finding someone I really cared about and who really cared about me. I had been settling, scared to be alone. Instead of letting him go, I would have stayed in a dead relationship. It might not have been bad or abusive, but it was indifferent.

"I'm glad it happened. Not the timing, but it made me realise that I was settling. I hope you find someone worth staying for." With that, I turn and grab Cain's hand. He's quiet as we walk towards our hideaway.

"What happened with you and him?" he asks once we are tucked away. I play with his fingers, unwilling to look at him. The stars shine above us and we are laid out underneath them again.

"When my parents,,," I take a breath, "died. We were going out, had been for a while. But I wasn't the same after, I just couldn't deal," I look away. "I needed him and he pulled away, and then I found out he had been cheating on me with Chrissy."

"How?"

"I was having a panic attack. I couldn't sleep and I needed to be held so I went to his unit and walked in on them. He told me he couldn't deal with all the attention and that I was different in that I didn't want to have fun anymore," I scoff.

"Are you kidding me?" Cain shouts. I look at him in surprise.

"You just lost your parents and he's mad because you didn't want to have fun? What an ass. You obviously needed him, he should have been there for you." He carries on ranting and I smile. I don't listen to his words but the anger on my behalf on his face undoes me. There are so many sides to Cain that I feel like I'm finding. He's not what I expected. He stops shouting, his mouth shutting as he looks at me.

"What?" He asks gruffly.

"Thank you." He looks confused.

"For what?" His voice is quieter now.

"Understanding." His face softens.

"I didn't realise at first, but I kept replaying it in my head. She looked so smug. I just don't know why she hates me," I voice the nagging thought that's been bothering me awhile.

"She wants what you have. It's because she's jealous of you," he says, like it's obvious.

"What do you mean?" I look at him in confusion.

"For someone so smart, you are dumb sometimes." He laughs as I sputter. "She's jealous of you, most of the girls our age on board are. You're effortlessly beautiful, they spend hours on their hair and makeup and you rock up, having just gotten out of bed, looking amazing. You don't care what anyone thinks and you're smart as hell. You think yourself out of situations and act like an adult, not a kid playing adult. You don't dumb yourself down to get attention, hell, half of the time you don't even realise you have it. Barrott, the two new kids and," he looks at me seriously. "Me. You've had me chasing after you since our first race. I could go on forever, but the point is you're an adult while they are still children. They notice, especially Chrissy; it's obvious she's jealous of you." I don't know what to say, I just stare at him.

He looks back at me and I see his gaze drop to my lips. He leans in and I know I should pull away, but I don't want to. I want him to kiss me. I missed feeling like a teenage girl and I know Cain would never take advantage. I want to remember our kiss this time. His lips barely touch mine when a siren blares to life. We jump apart and leap up. I look at him in confusion.

"What is that?" I shout to be heard over it. He shakes his head and grabs my hand. I follow him as we go to see what's happened.

We run into Barrott in one of the hallways. Streams of guards are running past us when he spots us. He yanks me to the side and waits for them to go past.

"Why aren't you in your unit?" he growls. I pull my arm from his, still hurt over his words. He looks at Cain and then his eyes drop. Barrott looks pained as he looks at my hand in Cain's, but he glances back up quickly and wipes it away like it was never there.

"What's going on?" I ask, the volume of the siren lowered, leaving just the red lights flashing in every corridor.

"I have to go." He looks at Cain. "Get her home and stay there with her until the siren stops." He goes to leave, and I grab his arm.

"What is going on?" I ask louder. He looks around and then back at me.

"Rebels." With that, he runs after the other guards. *Wait, as in the rebels caused the siren? How would they do that?*

"Come on Indy." Cain pulls me after him, the mood sombre as we watch everything on our way to my unit. The hallways are deserted, it's weird. We don't see a single person. We lock the door to my unit, and I start to pace around. Cain is stretched out on my sofa, watching me with a bemused look.

"Sit down Indy, before you wear through the steel." I stop and look at him, my hands on my hips.

"What did he mean rebels? How did they cause the alarm?" I nibble on my lower lip. "I need to know what's happening." He sighs and leans forward, resting his elbows on his knees.

"What do you know about the rebels?" he asks gently. I narrow my eyes at him.

"What do you know?" I shoot back. He pats the spot beside him, and reluctantly I sit down.

"Just what I overheard from my father. Apparently, the attacks started small,,,"

"Attacks?" I shout. He shushes me.

"Attacks. They are starting fires, damaging property, and in the process, the ship. That's why the guards are pulling doubles as well as the engineers." *The accidents,* I think with a gasp. Wait, Barrott is out there, what if he gets hurt? My heart nearly stops at that. I might be mad at him, but I still care.

"Why?" I ask instead. Cain shrugs.

"All I heard was they are claiming they fight for the truth."

I sigh and rub my head, a headache forming.

"Do you think Barrott will be okay?" I ask, concerned. He snorts.

"That man is like the Terminator. Ain't no hurting him, speed demon." I nod, he's right, I know he's right.

"Can I ask you something?" he asks hesitantly.

I focus on his face again and nod.

"Are you and him...?" He trails off, watching me.

I tilt my head.

"No." All I'm willing to give him. He offers me a wide smile.

"Good." He tangles his hand through mine and we spend the rest of the siren talking. Him more than me, he keeps my mind busy with funny stories and when the siren stops, I'm actually laughing. He says goodnight, then disappears, and I'm left with my thoughts.

First Effie, and now Chrissy, accusing me of having four men. When did my love life get so complicated? Effie! I jump up and race to the comms unit. I call her housing unit again and again until eventually, she answers. Her hair is disheveled, and she's in her pyjamas.

"Indy?" She asks around a yawn. I slump, the tension running out of me.

"You okay?" I ask her. She nods and scrubs her eyes.

"Are you? What's up?"

"Just the siren, I just wanted to check that you are okay. Go back to sleep." She nods, still half asleep, and says a tired goodbye.

I head back to the sofa and pick up a book, but I read the same page ten times before I chuck it down with a huff. I try watching a film but I'm too distracted. I need to know Barrott's okay. The brothers said they were stopping at home, so I'm betting they're fine. The siren was on this level after all. He's the only one I don't know about, I won't be able to sleep without knowing.

All my anger and hurt floats away with the thought that he could be hurt. I resume my pacing from earlier. It's another half an hour before the buzzer at my door goes. I rush over and open it. Barrott stands on the other side looking exhausted, but unhurt. I jump at him and he wraps his arms around me. I cling to him like a monkey, but he doesn't complain. He just walks into my unit, carrying me. I eventually let go and run my eyes over him.

"You okay?" I need to be sure. His lips quirk at me. He pushes me down to the sofa and follows, sitting next to me.

"I'm fine. Is that kid gone?" he asks gruffly. I slap his chest lightly.

"He's not a kid, and yes," I grumble. He grabs my hand and holds it to his chest, his heart beating against my palm, reassuring me better than his words. He leans his head back against the sofa and closes his eyes.

"So, the rebels?" I ask lightly, making him groan.

"I don't wanna talk about it," he grumbles. I nod and look anywhere but at him. Now that I know he's okay, the hurt is returning. I don't know how, but he must realise it, because he cracks his eyes open and looks at me. With a sigh, he sits up and turns to face me.

"Indy, what I said yesterday. I didn't mean it. I was just mad and tired, and I took it out on you." He watches my face closely.

"So, I'm not a burden?" I joke but it falls flat. He frowns and then grabs me, putting me on his lap. He wraps his arms around me and leans his head against mine where it's resting against his chest.

"Never Inds. I don't know what I would do without you." I sit there a while, letting him hold me.

"So the kid..," He trails off. I smile against his chest, content to be in his arms even if it means something different for both of us.

"Not a kid," I remind.

"Fine, the not kid. You two dating?" he asks casually, but I feel his body tense.

"No."

He lets out a breath. I never lie to Barrott though.

"We've just been hanging out, but I like him." He tenses again, his whole body hardening like steel.

"You do?" His voice is deep and full of emotion.

"I do." He flinches like I've struck him. I lean my head back and look at his face. His eyes are downcast and his face is full of pain. It's now or never. I need to know.

"Why do you care?" I ask, watching him intently.

"Because I look after you and I don't want you to get hurt again." But he won't look at me and I feel like he's left something out.

"We promised to never lie to each other, so why are you now?" I demand, crossing my arms under my breasts. He rubs his forehead and then looks at me. He leans back, me still perched on his lap. I go to scoot off, feeling weird, but he locks me there with his arms.

"Because you don't want to know the truth." He stares at me as he says it.

"What-" His radio goes of cutting off, what I was going to say. He stares at me as he answers it.

"Yeah?" He says gruffly.

"Sir, we need you in command."

"Understood, on my way." I get off his knee. He brushes my cheekbone gently.

"Go to sleep, Indy. I'll see you later." I nod, watching him leave again, hoping one day he will stop running.

"Be careful," I call after him.

<hr />

TRANSMISSION LOG 00308
DATE: 2033
MISSION: 43, COLONY
SHIP: DAWNBREAKER
DESTINATION: AYAMA

>............... Accepted
> Last night, the rebels targeted the guard
quarters. A few have serious injuries, the
others minor. Workers are starting to ask questions as the rebels get braver. Please advise
on how to proceed?

CHAPTER EIGHT

DAY 919

WITH FLYING training still cancelled and Effie busy in the medical centre, I'm bored out of my fucking mind. Barrott is off doing god knows what and Cain is in the upper which I don't have access to. So, I'm laying on the sofa feeling sorry for myself. Wait, I haven't heard from the brothers since before the siren. Jumping up, I head to the comms unit. When I get there I hesitate, they never told me their unit number. I nibble on my lip in thought. I guess it might be on the registry though?

I scroll through the units and names, looking for a familiar one. When none stick out, I get annoyed. I never even asked their last name, some friend I am. I look through the other options when I spot 'recent.'

Opening it, I see the news from inside the ship. There, at number twenty, is a mechanics promotion, it's got to be their dad. His last name is listed so I go back over to the unit listings and find it. While it rings, I do a happy dance to myself. It rings and rings and no one answers. Trying again, I start to get worried. I know they had today off so why wouldn't they answer? They still don't answer after my third attempt, so I grab my jacket and jog out of the door, intent on finding my boys.

I'll check their unit first and then the lagoon. I make my way through the twisting halls and down a level, counting the units as I go. Their unit is one of the last before the levels of the lowers. I press their buzzer and wait, my nerves eating me up. When no one answers, I press it again. It slides open to reveal an older man in a dirty tank top and the standard mechanic trousers. I take a step back from the fury on his face. He looks like the brothers, apart from his grey hair and his eyes the eyes that have crows feet around them, but he has the same face.

"Mr. Basford?" I inquire in a nervous voice.

"Who the fuck is asking?" He looks me up and down and I flinch from the leer he throws at me.

"I'm looking for Auden and Eldon." He snorts, which makes his belly jiggle in an unattractive way.

"I don't know where them good for nothing boys are. If you find them, you tell them I'm looking for them." He goes to step back but looks me up and down again.

"You get bored of those kids and need a real man, you come to me." He slams the door shut and I'm left gaping at the metal. I knew their dad was an asshole, but still.

I head to the lagoon hoping I can find them there, if not, I'll have to search all the common areas which will take forever. When I reach the lagoon, I stand at the door looking around, my eyes desperately seeking them. There's a man swimming and a woman seated on the beach. I stop when I notice two bodies side by side, sitting at the end of the jetty. I know it's them. Happiness bursts in my chest as I hurry their way, kicking off my shoes and jacket as I go. They don't even acknowledge me when I stand behind them. I lay one hand on each of their shoulders and they jump.

"It's me, guys. I've been looking for you," I say cheerfully. Auden's shoulders hunch and Eldon doesn't say anything. I sit behind Auden, wrap my arms around his back, and lean my head on it.

"You two okay?" I ask, slightly worried at their reactions. Auden starts to shake in my arms.

"Guys, you're freaking me out. I went to see your dad and-" Eldon shoots up, towering above me, his hands clenched into fists.

"Did he hurt you?" he shouts. My eyes go wide and then I spot the bruise along the top of his forehead. I jump up and reach to gently touch it. He lets me, but his face is still dark with anger.

"Tell me he didn't touch you?" His voice is deep, and his eyes beg me to prove that the monster hasn't hurt me.

"He didn't, he made a few advances that's about it. Did he do this?" I go to touch it again and he catches my hand.

"It's fine," he mutters, deflating now that he knows I'm okay. I yank my arm back, getting angry.

"Like fuck it is. Did he do this to you?" I ask louder. He grinds his teeth, but doesn't respond. I spin to Auden and grab his shoulder, pulling him to face me. He closes his eyes, but I can still see the pain and embarrassment on his face. He has a black eye and a split lip. My emotions turn deadly at the damage to his face. I whirl back to Eldon.

"Did. He. Do. This?" I enunciate every word. He nods and looks at the ground. I look at them both, they are ashamed. I push my anger down for later, knowing that right now they need me calm. I turn to Auden and kneel, he's looking everywhere but at me. I brush my lips under his eye and then gently over his split lip.

"Come on, cutie." I grab his hand, standing, and let him make the decision. He stands slowly and clutches my hand like he's scared I will leave. Eldon looks at his brother, the pain clear on his face. I step forward, still holding Auden's hand, brace myself on Eldon's chest, and lean on my tiptoes. I wait there, letting him make the decision like I did with his brother. He eventually tilts his head down where I can reach. I brush my lips over his bruise and then step back.

"Let's go watch a movie, okay?" My voice sounds weird to me, but they don't seem to notice. They nod and follow after me. Their silence, more than anything else, breaking my heart. I miss my happy boys. I lead them back to my unit where they fall asleep curled up on either side of me halfway through the movie as I stroke their hair and whisper funny stories in their ears. The whole time, the fury has been burning in my blood and a plan was forming in my head. When I'm sure they are asleep, I slip out of their arms and make my way to the medical centre.

"Hey, you looking for Effie?" One of the doctors asks, I recognize him but don't care at the moment. I nod, if I open my mouth I might scream.

"She was in one of the offices." He walks away to a patient with a distracted smile. Luck must be on my side. I leave the treatment rooms and head down the hallway to the offices. A few are busy, but I notice one with a doctor's name on it. I open the door and immediately lock it behind me. Shutting the privacy blinds as I head to the computer.

I use Effie's login and access the database. I look through the files and print what I need. Grabbing a folder, I shove the papers in before I log Effie out and quickly log myself in. I send a quick message over the comms before waiting anxiously for the reply, grinning when it pops through. I log out and leave the room. Stepping out of the office, I look around to see if anyone noticed. The hallway is empty. I don't rush, but I leave the medical wing, and make my way to the engineering wing my blood burning with every step.

I ignore all the others working there while looking for Howard. I find him bent over a table, plans and papers spread in front of him. Standing next to him, I wait for him to notice me. When he does, he looks confused.

"You okay, kiddo?" He rubs his head as he speaks.

"I need a favour." His eyebrows reach his hairline, but he nods straight away. I outline my plan and leave him to his work, the next step in my plan making me walk faster. I don't even see the hallways as I speed past. Instead, I concentrate on breathing deep and trying to stay in control, which is hard for someone who is notorious for having none, but for them? I'm willing to do anything. Effie was right. I let them in and now they are in deep. They took my pain as their own and offer me comfort when I need it. But right now, they need me, even if they don't know it.

I buzz on the door and hear shuffling and cursing. It slides open to his enraged face again. Good to know it's not just me he greets like that. He leers at me like he did earlier. I wonder if it is his go-to facial expression.

"Decide they are too young for you, sexy?" I swallow my disgust and paint a smile on my face.

"Yep."

He smirks and steps back, letting me in. I follow him, looking around as I step through the threshold. It's a hot mess. No wonder they don't want to live here. I turn and wait for him to shut the door. He looks at me, licking his disgusting lips.

"Did you know that they keep medical records from Earth?" I ask conversationally. He frowns, his blood clearly headed south.

"The fuck you on about?" He snarls.

"You see, I know you beat your sons and now I know you used to beat your wife. No wonder the poor woman left you, space doesn't change whether you are an abusive asshole or not. I have hers and their medical records here. They might have been overlooked, but if I go higher up and present them with evidence of your most recent beatings..." I tut. He grows redder, his eyes bugging out of his head. He might resemble the brothers, but the harshness to his face and the anger in his eyes are something that you would never see in Eldon and Auden.

"They won't just believe you, you stupid bitch!" I smile, all the disgust for this man evident in it. I've never hated someone so much before. Seeing what he did to them broke my heart. Worse yet was seeing the emotional repercussions. I would take on all the abusive assholes on board to see them smile again.

"I think they will. You see, I also have a couple of friends higher up. You are a mechanic, right? Well, it seems you are on your last strike there which is shocking, really, seeing as how you only just got promoted. Wouldn't it be a shame if someone found out about how you spend your credits on contraband?" I really owe Lee, I knew he was good for something.

"No one cares about that," he growls stepping closer to me.

"Not always, but add that to the evidence that you have been abusing your sons? Oh, they will want to make an example out of you." He laughs before descending into coughs, probably thanks to the vintage cigarettes he smokes.

"Sure, like they will believe some kid." My smile grows. He obviously doesn't like that and steps closer to backhand me. I flick my head back to him, ignoring the burning in my face and the ringing in my head. I laugh again, the movement pulling on my aching cheek. Damn, he might not be smart, but he hits like a rock.

"You're an idiot, see your gonna regret that. Not only do I have this evidence, but I also recorded your confession and you striking me." He stumbles back, his face paling when he realises the extent of what I will do, what I have already done.

"Did you think I was stupid enough to come here and confront you without backup? I knew they wouldn't believe me without proof. They have too much to deal with at the moment, and this is more hassle. But if I was to threaten this being leaked… well, they wouldn't want that. It would look bad on them, when at the moment, they need our support more than ever, especially if it was their darling orphan who leaked it." My smirk is fully grown now, and he looks green.

"Also helps I have a friend in the upper and one in the guards. They won't be happy when they see what you did to my face."

"What do you want?" he asks desperately.

"For you to be locked away for a long time. For you to never come near your sons again; never even look at them. But I know that no matter what you promise me, you simply won't keep it. It's in your nature. So, I will give you one chance. They will not be coming back here. They will stay with me. If you report them, or come after them, I will destroy you." I step closer after every threat I make.

"You will lose your job, your unit, your credits, your freedom and your passage to Ayama." Before me, the once big man shrinks, the weight of my threats crushing his shoulders.

"Okay, okay." He nods hard.

"Okay, what?" I say coldly.

"I won't go near them again or report them."

"Good," I turn to walk away before popping back around to look at him.

"Oh, and I'll be keeping the recording as well." I leave him there, looking terrified. I knew I needed to scare him away, in all honesty, I don't know if the uppers would've done anything. They are too busy trying to fight a rebellion but having that threat against him should stop him until something can be done. Feeling pleased with myself, I hum on the way back to my unit. At least now they are safe.

I'm still humming as I let myself into my unit. It dies when I see the living room. Eldon, Auden, Cain, and Barrott are all sitting there looking tense. Space balls.

"Hi guys, what's up?" I ask casually. I watch all their heads snap my way. Barrott growls and races to me when he sees my face, Cain and the brothers a step behind him. Cain looks furious, Eldon and Auden look resigned.

Barrott gently grips my face and turns it to the side, exposing my burning cheek. I'm betting I've got a nice little handprint.

"Who did this?" His voice is deeper than I've ever heard it, completely opposite to the gentle way he holds my tender face.

"Tell us," Cain demands. I ignore the man vibrating with barely leashed lethal intent in front of me and turn to the brothers.

"He will never hurt you again." They both stagger back, looking shocked.

"Anyone else hungry?" I ask sweetly.

———— ✧ ————

"You should've come to me," Barrott shouts. He's pacing in front of me and the brothers as we sit on the sofa. Auden is seated on my left, his hand clenched in mine. Eldon is to my right, holding the ice pack to my face. He worries me the most. He has withdrawn into himself since my declaration. He may be touching me, but he's a million miles away. Cain is sitting on the other sofa, watching it all unfold.

"And what would you have done? There's nothing you could do." Barrott yanks on his hair.

"Fucking hell, Indy I would have…" He trails off in a mutter. It must be bad if he's swearing.

"I couldn't allow him to hurt them anymore. What sort of person would that make me? I had to do something."

"But confronting him, someone you know who drinks and likes to beat on boys twice your size?" Auden flinches at Barrott's harsh words.

"Yes. I knew my plan would work," I say smugly.

"What if it didn't? Someone who is willing to hit his own sons is willing to do anything and you just threatened everything he cares about. What if he flipped and killed you!" He screams the last at me.

"It was a risk I was willing to take," I shrug and he stops in front of me, chest heaving, his face red from anger.

"You have serious balls, speed demon." I look at Cain as he offers me a smile. "Proud of you."

I smile back. Barrott turns his anger on him, and to Cain's credit, he doesn't even flinch.

"You are condoning this?" he snarls. Cain only leans back, crossing one leg over the other.

"No, but I will support her. Yes, I wish she had come to one of us beforehand, but I know she did what she thought she had to do. Are you telling me you wouldn't do something if you found out someone was hurting her?" Barrott fumes, pacing the living room. I let go of Auden's hand and stand before Barrott. I see the wildness in his eyes, I know it's because he couldn't protect me, my surly shadow. I stop his pacing by stepping in his way.

"I'm okay. Really. It wasn't even that hard. I had to do it, they're like my family. I wouldn't be me if I stepped back and did nothing." He frowns, but listens to me.

"I know you're mad. I'm sorry I didn't come to you before, but I thought you might stop me. I had to do this." He stares at me, his face stricken.

"You thought I would stop you?" he whispers.

"I thought you would try and change my mind. I knew following the rules on this one wouldn't work. Could you have promised me that if I reported it, the guards would have taken the time and had manpower to do anything?" I see the answer in his eyes, even if he doesn't want to say it

"I couldn't take that risk," I say softly. His face shutters.

"So, you risked yourself instead?" he growls.

"Yes. I would do the same for anyone, Cain and you included. I would do worse to make sure you were safe. I would do anything in my power, just like you would for me." I say the last without any embarrassment. His face softens, and he leans his forehead against mine, obviously forgetting about our spectators.

"I'm supposed to protect you. I'm supposed to stop anything from hurting you ever again. I can't go through that again with you," he mutters brokenly. I suck in a breath, knowing he's talking about my parents.

"I don't need you to protect me all the time, I just need you to support me. I need you here, with me. To always have my back," I whisper back. He takes a few deep breaths and closes his eyes, getting his emotions under control.

"Okay, but I'm still mad at you. It's a good thing I love you." I start to nod and then stop, frozen in shock. He obviously realises what he said and watches me carefully before pulling away and clearing his throat. He steps back and the usual Barrott returns, no ounce of softness or weakness on his face. He's got to be talking about *as a friend*, right? There's no way Barrott feels the same way I do?

"You will all stay here." He strides away without waiting for a response.

"Where are you going?" I ask.

"You just said what you would do for anyone who hurt me, do you not think I would do the same?" He's gone before I can respond.

I turn back to the others. Auden and Eldon aren't looking at me again. Cain stands and moves in front of me.

"I'm going to get us some food." He flicks his eyes to the brothers knowingly and I nod. He kisses my cheek. "You're amazing, babe." he whispers and then he's gone like Barrott.

I stand there, unsure.

"Are you mad at me?" I whisper, all my confidence is gone. Auden's head snaps up. He goes to speak, when Eldon interrupts.

"Yes," he's glaring at me. Auden looks from his brother to me. I step back in hurt.

"Why?" For some reason, I want to cry. I don't mind Barrott being mad at me, it's our usual, but the thought of these two being mad or even worse, disappointed in me, does me in. Eldon stands abruptly.

"You put yourself in danger. You left us here sleeping and went to him. You knew what he was capable of and you went anyway!" My eyes fill with tears at each angry word.

"Do you know what it was like waking up with you not in my arms anymore? Then you appear all happy with yourself with his handprint on your face!" he snarls. Auden stands slowly.

"Brother-" He is cut off by Eldon.

"No. We never asked for your help!" The tears drip down my face, but I start to get angry. I wipe them away with the back of my hand, not wanting them to see me weak.

"I know you didn't. I couldn't stand-"

"It wasn't for you to stand," he shouts. "You do not need to be in everyone's business." He storms off upstairs and I'm left with Auden. I look at the floor, the tears steadily falling. He wraps his arms around me.

"Thank you," he whispers. I grab his shirt and hold on, using him as my anchor while my heart aches.

"But Eldon-"

"He's mad that he wasn't there to protect you. He needs to cool down. He always tries to get between me and the blows. He thinks it's his responsibly, so the idea that you took a hit for him will break him. He's blaming himself right now for telling you. Without that, you might not have been struck." I breathe in his scent and burrow into his chest.

"I don't know how we got so lucky to have someone like you fighting for us, but never doubt our gratitude or feelings for you." I nod in his chest. He squeezes and steps back.

"Now, go see my brother before he destroys himself." I look at him in shock.

"But you just said he needs to calm down," I say softly.

"If there is anyone who can face his anger and self-hate, it's you. You just took down my father and soothed Barrott, you can handle him. Don't let him push you away. He needs you, Indy. He won't admit it and he will hate himself for the weakness, but he needs you. Like I needed to hold you to see for myself you were okay; so will he." He smiles gently at me and pushes me towards the stairs. Following his prompts, I slowly drag my feet as I head to see his brother.

I hesitate at the doorway. Eldon is sitting on my bed, his head in his hands. I breathe in and bolster my courage. He needs me. Even if it hurts me, I'll be there for him. Even when his anger is like a sword to my heart. I've never been so scared, not even when I faced the track or flew for the first time. The idea of losing him... I shake my head. It would kill something in me. In the short space of time I've known them, they have become part of my everything. I sit lightly next to him, my leg pressed against his, offering my support silently. I wait. I know he needs time, so I sit there patiently.

"I can't lose you," his whisper breaks halfway through, sending a stabbing pain through my chest. What else can you do but feel the pain when the one you care about does? Then I run his words through my head, it's not what I expected him to say. I stand up and he lifts his head. I kneel on the floor before him, between his parted legs. His face is streaked with tears and it makes my heart clench.

"You won't, not ever. You're stuck with me." I grab his legs and squeeze. His stares at me, looking so vunerable it sends my heart into overdrive, not in the least bit ashamed by his tears.

"But I nearly did, and I didn't even know." I lean my head against his leg. He runs his hand through my hair and I close my eyes.

"Promise me, Indy, promise that you won't do anything like that again." His voice is stronger. I open my eyes and let him see the truth.

"I can't promise that. What I can promise is next time, I'll try to come to you beforehand." He watches my face.

"Did I scare you?" he asks quietly. The change in conversation takes me a second to catch up.

"No, why?" I'm hoping I look as confused as I feel.

"I have my father's anger, Indy. I've always known it. I can usually push it down, but when I saw your face, I couldn't." Ah, so that's what was bugging him. Not that I pushed too much, but that he didn't like his reaction.

"You would never hurt me, Eldon," I declare, my voice strong, sure with the truth.

"You don't know that," he says softly, almost afraid to give the words life. Like letting out his darkest fear might make it real. But there's one thing he forgot. I don't run from things that scare me, I run to them.

"I do. You might yell, you might even make me cry, but you

would never lay a hand on me. That I know for sure. We all have anger, Eldon. I do; probably more than most. Losing my parents and then having to put up with everyone's reactions; it changed me. I snap easier, my anger is so volatile. I do stupid stuff, but it's about acknowledging it, and controlling it. I've only just started to acknowledge my reckless side, but now that I have, I understand why I do it. It makes me stop and think through things before I do them." He nods.

"Auden is softer, he never let the hate build in him," he offers sadly.

"So? Everyone reacts differently. I'm so goddamn happy with who you both are. You amaze me, that even after everything, you can laugh and joke and the men you have become? You are amazing. Both of you." I reach for his hand and still it, gripping it in mine. Showing him that I will lend him my strength when he has none.

"You mean it?" His voice is vulnerable.

"Always. When I look at you, I don't know how I got so lucky enough to have you in my life. Yet no matter how much I push, or how much you find out about me, you stick by my side. I don't know what I would do without you two. Before you came along, I was just existing. I'd stopped living, really living. Too afraid to let down my walls, then you two come in with your dimples, and contagious laughter, and changed everything." I offer him my heart and hope he doesn't stomp on it. He looks at me like I'm the light in his darkness.

"We are the lucky ones. Thank you for doing that for us. I didn't react well, but I truly am thankful. You changed us too, you might not see it, but I do." I smile at him and he smiles back. I stand up and crawl onto the bed behind him.

"Hold me?" I whisper in the darkening room.

"Forever." He curls up behind me and eventually, Auden comes in. He nods at his brother and offers me a brilliant smile and climbs in front of me. I hug him to me and I fall asleep in my favourite place, between two of the pieces of my heart. If only it wasn't split into four...

Someone shakes my shoulder. I groan and bury my head into something warm.

"Indy, wake up. You need to eat." I open one eye and look at Barrott's face.

"Come on," he whispers gently. I manage to get both arms out from around Auden and offer them up to Barrott sleepily. He smiles softly at me and shakes his head. He grabs my wrists and tugs until I'm standing at the edge of the bed. I hear a groan behind me.

"Food time boys," I yell and then jump up, wrapping myself around Barrott. He grunts, but catches me, holding me close. I look at the brothers as they both sit up instantly and eye me and Barrott up.

"Food?" Auden says happily. I grin and turn to Barrott, I kiss his cheek before hopping down and racing to the kitchen. Cain grins at me as I check out the food on the table. He grabbed enough for everyone. It's a strange mix of people for dinner, but it's the best one in a long time. We all sit around talking and joking and even Barrott joins in. I grin as I look around my makeshift family, all that's missing is Effie. I might have some things to figure out, like my feelings for each of them, but here and now, just being together is enough.

CHAPTER NINE

DAY 920

THEY ALL STAYED over at my unit last night. With me sharing the bed with the brothers and Barrott insisting to sleep on the floor. Eventually, Cain gave in and slept on the bedroom floor as well. Cain had left by the time I got up. I find Barrott in the kitchen, going over something on the comm unit.

"Morning," I mumble tiredly.

"Morning."

I round the table and sit down opposite him. He doesn't look up, which makes me frown.

"Everything okay?"

He nods before going back to looking at the unit.

"Oo-kay."

He sighs before pushing the unit away and looking at me. His eyes pierce mine, like a blow to my heart. There is so much swirling in them, I don't know where to begin.

"Barrott, what's wrong?" He looks down at the table; this silence is so unlike him. Standing, I round the table to his side and put my hand on his shoulder. He puts his hand over mine.

What the hell...

Using my foot I press on the switch just above the last rung on the chair, it instantly drops into some grooves in the floor making it easier to move. Using my foot still, I push the chair out and plop myself into his lap.

He grunts before his arms hesitantly wind around me. He pulls me closer and leans his head on mine as I snuggle into his chest. Breathing in his scent, I offer him comfort and wait to see if he will tell me what's wrong.

"I only worry because I care," he says softly, his breath moving loose strands of hair on my head. I fiddle with his shirt before flattening it and smoothing the material down.

"I know." His arms tighten before he rubs his head on mine.

"We are more alike than you know. You're my only family, Inds. I can't afford to lose you." His voice breaks, and he clears his throat. I think his words through. I'm his only family? I guess I never thought about it, I just figured he had his parents on Earth. Does he mean they are dead? Or that he doesn't talk to them?

"I'm terrified that I am going to wake up one day to find you gone, just like-" I lift my head, and he buries his head in my shoulder.

Hesitating, my hands gently drop to his head, and when he doesn't move, I run my fingers through his short hair.

"Hey, I'm not going anywhere. You will always have me. I will always be your family. Just like you are mine." He nods into my shoulder, but doesn't move. We sit there holding each other before he pulls away with a disappointed sigh.

"Promise me something?" he asks. His warm hand cups my cheek, making me close my eyes in bliss as I lean in closer. Blushing, I pull away; what the hell am I doing?

"Anything," I say, trying to cover for my awkwardness.

"Just promise me, no matter what, you won't ever push me away. That you will always need me." He finishes the last on a whisper. I can see the wetness in his eyes, also the fear.

"Barrott, I will always need you. I don't know how I would have survived my parents dying, or this year, without you. If I'm ever scared or need someone, I know you will always be there. I might not always say it, and seem ungrateful, but I would be lost without you." Taking a deep breath, I face him, showing my cards "You're my everything."

He sucks in a breath, searching my face. I don't know what he sees, but he drops his hand and his face closes down. My heart stutters as pain runs through my chest at him closing me away.

"Not anymore, I'm not." He gets up, causing me to stand as he walks to the door.

He can't keep doing this! Walking away and leaving me hurting. First, he says he loves me, then he shows me he's scared of losing me? But he's unwilling to move, this stubborn man!

"That's it? You're just gonna open up then walk away like it never happened? Why are you so scared of showing me any feelings, of just being with me for one moment without pretending it's your duty. Just be honest with yourself, because you sure as shit aren't with me!"

He stops with his back still to me.

"Have you ever thought that maybe the idea of opening up, of showing you how I feel, terrifies me? That the idea you could walk away from me kills me? I can live with you loving someone else, as long as I still get to be in your life. I can't live with having you and losing you, so we both need to move on from these feelings because that is what is happening here. I can see it already changing, changing you. You will have them, and I will find someone else, but I need some space to do that. It's all I could think about last night, running every possible scenario through my head only to lose you every time. I'm sorry Indy, but this is for the best."

He walks out before I can answer, and honestly, I don't know what I would say. It seems like every step forward we take, something blocks us, and we take two steps back. The chasm opening up between us with unsaid things and emotions will be our downfall. How long can I keep hoping he will realise he's what I want? What does he mean about moving on and space? How long before he pushes me away for good?

Tears slowly drip down my face, did he mean he won't be in my life anymore? The idea of him with someone else has me feeling sick. I don't think I could watch it. Which means that I would have to cut him out of my life. Sitting down at his empty seat, I drop my head into my hands. What am I going to do? Choose him and lose the brothers and Cain, or lose him and have them? Either option will break my heart. How can he do this to me, and expect me to be okay with this!

My heart nearly stops. Was this his way of saying goodbye? Was he holding me so tight because he was planning on letting me go? Pain has me gasping as I try to convince myself he wouldn't do that. I survived losing my parents, and as wrong as it sounds, I don't think I could survive losing him.

Time rushes past as I sit, lost in my own head trying to think of a way to make him understand, to not have to lose anybody. I don't have answers, and my heart still hurts at the way we have left things. I need my best friend.

Leaving the brothers sleeping, I go on a mission to find Effie. Now that my adrenaline rush is over and I'm trying not to think about Barrott, I feel bad about using her logins. If anyone traced it, she could be in some serious trouble. Plus I haven't seen her much recently, she's been so busy with her training, I need to talk to her about everything that has happened.

I'm lost in my thoughts when I almost run into two people in the hallway, I blink and mumble an apology while trying to step around them. When they move to block me again I lift my head with a glare.

In front of me is the bald man and the black-haired lady from the race.

"What?" I snap. They look behind me with a nod. I turn and see two men with their arms crossed blocking the hallway behind me. I turn back to the ones who are obviously in charge.

"What do you want?" I ask slowly.

"Just to talk," the woman says, her voice is high and annoying.

"You brought two goons with you just to talk?" I scoff in disbelief. She smiles, but it doesn't reach her eyes. The bald-headed man is giving me the creeps; he's so silent and there's something about him that screams at me to run the other way.

"They are simply here to make sure no one gets hurt," she says, the fake smile in place.

"And why would someone get hurt?" My voice is even and I'm proud of myself.

"Let us go somewhere more private, Indy."

I narrow my eyes at her.

"No," I cross my arms and mimic the goons' stance. Her brow furrows like she's not used to being denied.

"No?" She echoes.

"No. You can say whatever you want to say here."

She looks behind me and shakes her head, but I don't move my eyes off her, she's the one in charge after all.

"I didn't want to do it this way, Indy. Please know I really do just want to talk." Something smashes into the back of my skull and sends me tumbling into the waiting darkness.

MOTHERFUCKER, my head is killing me!

It feels like I drank a whole crate of Lee's moonshine. I lift my hand to rub the back of it; when I feel a bandage there, I freeze. What the hell? Cracking open my eyes, I quickly slam them shut again when the light spears painfully into them, causing a painful throb in my already aching head.

"Go steady." A woman's voice instructs, the high pitch of it grating on my already sensitive head. I do what she says though; I wait for the throbbing to fade to a dull ache, and then I slowly open my eyes again, giving them time to adjust to the light. My head is resting on my chest, and when I tilt it up, my neck protests. I'm guessing I have been slumped like that for a while. I crack my neck from side to side while surveying the room I'm in. There is a metal table in front of me and it looks like we are in a housing unit, except its only one room and the table, a chair opposite me and the one I am sitting on is the only furniture in the room.

"What, not bothering to tie my hands down?" I joke, covering the pain in my voice.

"That won't be necessary, Indy. After all, like I said I just want to talk."

I crane my neck around to look for her. She steps out from behind me and gracefully sits on the chair opposite me.

"Then why do I feel like I'm in an interrogation room? Oh my god, is it probing time?" I gasp dramatically, and she recoils in disgust.

"Please, Indy, we have some very important matters to discuss; it involves your parents." She crosses her legs, her words instantly sobering me.

"What about my parents?" I snarl. She raises one perfectly plucked eyebrow at me.

"We will get to that in time. Now, as I was saying-"

"No, I think we will get to that now," I say and lean back in my chair mirroring her. She frowns at me, anger flashing across her face before she forces the fake smile back.

"Of course. Your parents were the ones who started this, after all."

"Started what?" I ask in confusion, I don't know whether the blow to the head is making me slow or she is being purposely vague.

"The rebellion, of course. We are The Saviours, Indy, and we need your help."

Well, shit, I wasn't expecting that. My head gives a painful throb as if to say 'me too'. I just stare at her dumbly.

"You are telling me my parents started the rebellion?" My voice is as incredulous as I feel. My straight-laced parents? She lifts one shoulder and drops it.

"In a way. I am a scientist too; I worked with your mother. She was working on the life cycle of Ayama. Studying the new planet, from the life of the smallest cell to the outcome from our colonisation. She found something, she took it to the higher-ups but they dismissed her and told her to move on from her work to something else. She did not, she carried on looking."

"What did she find?" She stares at me, watching me like a hawk.

"Ayama is dying, our changes to the air, hell to even the plant life, are killing the planet. We didn't learn from our mistakes, we are doing it all over again but this time it looks like the effect on the planet is sped up. The uppers and government don't want us to know that. Can't let a ship full of colonists know they are heading for a dying planet, right?"

"You've got to be kidding me," I laugh bitterly.

"I'm afraid not." She looks at me sadly, but it's like a mask. It's not quite right; it's just a little off, like someone trying to imitate the emotion.

"How would they not know the planet was dying? Do you really expect me to believe they are stupid enough to think this will stay under wraps?"

"Desperate people do desperate things. They are planning on informing certain people when we get there. There is already a team on the ground working on saving the planet, on reversing the effect of humans habitating a world we shouldn't."

"How do you know all of this?" My voice is full of scorn.

"I am one of the people on the team hoping to save the planet."

"And instead of doing that, you decided to start a rebellion?"

"The people have a right to know, Indy. This is practically a suicide mission; the chances of us being able to save the planet are slim!"

"Who knows?" I ask, anger growing in my belly. If Barrott or Cain knew and didn't tell me, I don't think I will be able to forgive them. This woman's methods might be wrong, but she has a point: the people have the right to know. But won't that cause a panic? Work and training would stop, and we would be in a tin can in space as people riot. Maybe the uppers have a good idea with only telling a certain amount of people until they know more. The moral debate causes a jackhammering in my head, which I have to breathe through.

"Not many, the main crew, the head guards and a few select scientists." I breathe a sigh of relief, so Cain shouldn't know, but what about Barrott?

"So, your solution to make them tell everyone is to hurt the ship and the people on board?" I scowl at her, remembering the people in the medical centre.

"Every cause has its share of innocent blood spilt. We are showing the uppers we are serious in our threats. They must inform the ship, or we will keep going."

"You could disable the ship, and then we would be stuck in space!" I shout.

"No, we have the best people as part of the rebellion, we know exactly where to hit and what sort of damage the ship can take."

"You are going about this wrong," I say, looking into her eyes. Anger flares in her the brown depths, but I carry on. "If what you say is true, the people deserve to know or have the right to choose; I agree with you on that. But instead, you are starting a war with the uppers and only hurting everyone in the process. You aren't helping; you are using this knowledge as an excuse to rain anarchy down on this ship. You say your people know where to hit. What if they are wrong? What if you damage the ship? What if you kill someone? It won't make people trust you. In fact, it will do the opposite. You will push them away, and then they will never believe you. They will think you are the problem and this rebellion is a way to hurt them. You are letting your anger cloud your judgment, and it's making you blind. Your original goal is gone, and instead, your anger at the division between classes is becoming more and more apparent. Let me ask you this. Are you really fighting because you think the people deserve the truth or because it is a good excuse to get back at the uppers because of who and what they stand for?"

I try to get my thoughts across without rambling. I think of Cain and try to convey to her the wrongness of their judgement.

"Not everyone up there is bad, just like not everyone down below is good. You can't blame them for your social level. When we get to Ayama, it won't matter; you can start again, be who you want. But this rebellion will cause more damage than good if you continue the way you are going, and no one will be left to save the planet you claim is dying."

I take a deep breath, proud of myself for standing up to them and trusting logic even when hurt and anger swirl inside of me. Why didn't my parents tell me? Why would they keep something like this from me? Did it lead to their death?

Her face turns pensive. She eyes me like she's never seen me before.

"Is that your final decision?" she asks coldly. I sigh and lean back, the words having obviously floated over her head.

"There wasn't a decision to make. You never even told me why you need me?" The throb in my head is back bigger than ever, and all I want to do is curl up in bed with the brothers.

"You are not ready to know, if that's how you feel." She stands and goes to leave without another word.

"So, are you planning on keeping me here?" I scoff. She doesn't even turn to look at me.

"You may leave, although I wouldn't suggest talking to anyone about what happened here. You should know this rebellion is bigger than you can imagine and those you hold dear might not be the people you think they are." I look at the table trying to breathe through the agony racing through my veins. "We will make you understand how serious we are, then you will help us. If only you knew how important you were." With that cryptic threat, she is gone. Great. I go to stand, but have to sit back down when my head spins. Did they really need to hit me?

CHAPTER TEN

DAY 920

UNSURE WHAT TO DO, I search the ship for Barrott, needing answers only he can provide. I know we left everything in a bad place with me not sure where we are, but I know if I need him he will be there. He also knows the most about the rebellion, and it's got me wondering how.

I search everywhere but the crew quarters, gradually getting more and more frustrated. When I spot a man following me each turn I take, I start to get worried. When I spot the same man again when I turn the next corner I start to panic. That woman trusted me with a lot of secrets and, I did see her face. It makes sense she would have me watched. It means I can't just bumble around the ship screaming "coup!".

My head is throbbing at me, a reminder of the blow I sustained, so I decide to give up and head back home. I'll message Barrott and hope that he gets it quickly. I don't see anyone on the way back to my unit, thank god. When I stumble inside, I lay on the sofa thinking through everything she said. My head is agony at this point and the room is dimming to black. I try to fight it but my body shuts down. Too much stress, too much pain. Just too much.

When I wake up, my eyes are blurry and the pain in my head is dulled. Shit, how long was I out? Did I even send a message to Barrott? Flinging myself off the sofa in confused panic, I head to the comms unit. The screen is hazy and it's a lot more difficult than it should be to access it.

I can't go on like this, but if I go to the med bay they will ask questions. My sluggish brain takes a while before I decided to message Effie to see if she will come check me out. It does pay to have a healer as a friend. When she doesn't reply straight away, I grumble and decide to shower, at least it might wake me up.

After the quickest shower in history, I wipe the condensation away from the glass and wince at my haggard appearance. My head throbs, reminding me of my injury and I poke the lump on the back of it experimentally. When pain lances through my head I wince and drop my hand. Pushing away from the mirror, I slowly get dressed, having to focus on each task more than normal. By the time I'm in my jumpsuit, I'm panting and exhausted. Great.

I slowly head back to the comms unit to check if Effie has messaged me. Three messages await and I tap the top one.

Meet us in the lagoon, good looking :)

Smiling a little, I tap the next.

Speed Demon, something is wrong, just lay low for now okay?

Frowning, I consider his warning. What the hell is going on in this ship? The next message pops up.

I'll be there in the next hour.

No sender, which means it's Barrott. Good, at least I might get some answers. I try to ignore my heart speeding up at the thought of seeing him again. There are much more important things than my unanswered questions about our relationship. I'm just turning away when it goes off again.

Sure thing babe, be at yours in five. Is everything okay?

I quickly type my response.

Yes, but bring your med bag.

Ignoring the chime from her response, I drag my ass to the sofa and slump there, waiting for her. Can today get any worse?

"YOU REALLY NEED to go to the medical bay, Inds," Effie pleads as she paces in front of me. I groan and get comfy on the sofa, wincing at the pressure on the back of my sore head. The door buzzes and she throws me a dirty look as she keeps talking on her way to answer it.

"I mean it, you could have seriously damaged your brain. Not that there's much up there but still--"

Her words cut off in a gasp which has me sitting bolt upright. My head spins for a second at moving too fast.

"INDY!" Her scream cuts off in a muffle and I throw myself off the sofa. Swaying on unsteady feet, I squint at the person at the door. What the-

The brother's dad is standing in front of the closed door, two men spread out behind him. His palm is over Effie's mouth as she struggles in his grip.

With a creepy smile at me, he pushes her across the room, away from him. She lands hard on the floor and scrambles over to me, tears trekking down her face. When she reaches me, I pull her behind me. She grabs my arms and hides there. Panic races through my veins, making my already weak body shake.

"Did you really think you would get away with it bitch? Threatening me and then sending your dog after me?" He sneers as he steps closer. The men at his back don't move from the door. They are big, bigger even than Barrott. Jumpsuits cover their barrel chests and they must be in their mid-forties. No expression covers their thick faces, as if this is just another day at work for them.

"My dog?" I ask in confusion as I step back, pushing Effie with me. When he gets closer, I gasp at what is left of his face. The whole left side is black and blue, with the odd purple mixed in. His nose is obviously broken and his other eye is sealed shut. He leans to one side as he walks and winces, letting me know his body is probably no better. His left arm, the one he didn't touch Effie with, is covered from elbow to wrist in a gel healer. The blue liquid and nanobots working to fix the damage. It must have been extensive for them to still be working.

"That little guard of yours," he snarls. My heart clenches; oh Barrott, what did you do?

"I didn't know- I didn't." I stop when he laughs, the sound horrible and grating.

"Don't pretend you, little whore. Not only have you got my sons' pussy-whipped, you have that fucking piece of shit guard. Is your little cunt made of gold or something? Maybe I'll see before I leave you as a message for them." He grabs his crotch as he eyes me. Plans and escape routes run through my head, the odds not good. I don't see a way I'm getting out of this, but I won't let him touch Effie. I won't let her pay for my mistake.

"Let the healer leave." My voice is steady, which I'm proud of. Even though bile is creeping up my throat at the thought of him touching me.

"Healer?" he asks curiously.

"The girl behind me, she's a healer. I called her here to check my head out." Effie goes to speak behind me, but I pinch her arm, making her yelp.

"So, not another one of your friends?" He sniggers over the last word as he wanders closer to me again.

"I don't even know her. But if you hurt a healer, you will face the death penalty," I warn him casually, trying not to convey how important it is he lets her go. If I show interest, he will use her against me. He cocks his head in thought as he tries to see behind me to her. One of the men at the door steps forward.

"She's right." He throws a slightly dirty look at the brother's dad which makes him hunch his shoulder before nodding at him. As he turns back around, I nod at the man in thanks.

He slightly inclines his head before going back to looking bored. So, they might not help me, but they will help get Effie out and they are obviously here as muscle and have some sort of pull over him?

"Fine, I don't want her anyway. Let the healer bitch out." He waves his hand before turning back to me.

I grab Effie's arm and pull her around to my side, the furthest away from him. I slowly walk past, dragging her every step.

"Indy-" she whispers, the sound full of unshed tears.

I don't bother to reply, but I stand before the men at the door.

"I wouldn't tell anyone what is going on if I was you, you never know when someone is watching." He narrows his eyes in meaning at her, and hers widen. I nod my head in understanding of the warning then push her to the door. She stumbles and turns back to me.

"In-"

I cut her off with a fake glare.

"Go back to the lagoon where I found you, healer, and don't tell anyone."

I'm hoping that's where the boys are, but it's the most I can do with them all watching me. I know she won't get back to me in time before he hurts me, but the brothers will protect her. Stepping back, I'm slammed into a doughy chest. Holding in my gag at the arms that wrap around me, I watch my best friend as she crumbles. Her face is red and covered in tears, her lips pinched in her distress. As I watch, she regains her composure, and with one last look, whirls and steps out of the closing door. With her goes all of my chance to escape.

I watch as the steel closes, blocking me from the rest of the ship. Leaving me at the mercy of a madman. I don't know how long I stand staring before he gets bored. His hand winds through my hair tenderly before yanking. I'm dragged back to the living room by it, shouts of pain escaping my surprised mouth.

He lets me go in front of the sofa, my head banging painfully on the cold floor from the force of it. My eyes blur from the pain jackknifing through my head. I don't even have time to suck in a breath before he's on me. All my training with Barrott goes out the window as he pins me to the floor. Panic has my body jerking beneath him, trying to get free. He backhands me, my cheek instantly flaring with agony. The distraction is enough to still my movements so he can lower his body on mine.

His foul breath hits my face as I turn away from his descending head. My raw cheek presses into the floor, the coldness cooling some of the sting.

"I'm going to have some fun with you, girl. When my sons find you, there will be nothing left but a broken and used body."

Tears fill my eyes and I scrunch them closed as his hands wander along my body. He squeezes a breast before moving on, the feeling leaving slime in his wake. My chest heaves with the horror of what is happening as my adrenaline surges through me.

"They'll know who it was." My voice is weak and trembling and my warning only makes him laugh harder.

"Oh, I'm not worried, bitch. Everyone's a little too preoccupied at the minute to care about one little orphan." My head snaps around to him.

"What's happening?" My horror retreats as my curiosity gets the better of me. His hands still, one over my breast, one along my rib cage.

"Who knows? Some cunt told me everyone would be busy, so to have my fun. She even sent these men here to make sure 'nothing gets out of hand' but what that stupid old bitch doesn't know won't hurt her." He grins at the last, his sour breath hitting my face again.

"Long black hair?" Why the fuck am I questioning him?

"Yes, now enough questions," he snarls the last as his hand squeezes painfully, causing tears to gather in my eyes again. My mind is half focused on the here and now and the other half on what he said. Why would the rebel leader pass on information? She wanted my help, so what changed? Maybe she saw me as too much of a threat. I frown in concentration. Or maybe it doesn't matter anymore.

My head rocks to the side with another hard slap.

"Pay attention, cunt."

My mind refocuses, none of my speculation matters if I can't get out of this mess. I start to struggle again, but it's no use; he's too big and it only seems to spur him on. He grabs my cheeks to slam my head down on the floor. The pain rocks through my abused head, making me scream. When my eyes focus again he's grinning down at me.

"Let's see how magical this cunt is, shall we?" I hear movement from the men at the door, like they are shuffling uncomfortably.

"The agreement was that you get to rough her up, and the rebellion gets to send a message about denying their requests." The voice is hesitant but strong.

His head snaps up as he glares their way. His mouth opens to say something when the floor rocks underneath us. A massive bang sounds as it rocks again, sending him flying off me. Using the distraction, I scramble to my feet with my back to the wall.

The ship rocks again, the sound of metal screaming reaching us. I stumble, but use the wall for support. The floor tilts as the ship moves, harshly jerks up, sending the brothers' dad flying across it. Eyeing the door, I make my bid for escape. The floor moves dangerously beneath me as explosions so loud I have to cover my ears go off. I hop over his prone figure and then slide across the floor to the other men. They are both clutching the wall, holding on for dear life as the ship jars and spins beneath us. I smash my hand against the screen and wait for the agonisingly slow moments it takes to turn green.

"Fucking stop her!" he shouts from behind me, but I'm already squeezing through the gaps in the opening door. Once on the other side, I slam my hand down again, locking them in.

CHAPTER ELEVEN

DAY 920

STUMBLING AWAY FROM THE DOOR, I look around wildly. The corridor is empty and the lights flash red, throwing the hallway into a semblance of darkness. A siren starts up, only to be interrupted by the sounds of the constant explosions. Screaming reaches me as guns go off in the distance. My muddled brain panics as I look around. The ship is obviously damaged. That means I need to get to an emergency shuttle. My training kicks in as I whirl and run down the corridor, sliding and nearly slipping at least once. At the intersection, I stop. My brain is hurting so bad but I push it back and try to remember why I am hesitating.

Effie! Shit, the guys!

Hesitating for only a moment longer, I spin turn away from the corridor that would lead me to the emergency shuttles. The noise of fighting dies out the further away from the shuttles I get until it's deadly quiet apart from my heavy breathing. The lights blink out above me, casting the corridor into an eerie red as the lights strobe above me. The light barely pierces the darkness, making me squint and stretch my arms out so I don't bump into anything. With a cry, I'm flung into the wall as the ship banks again. My shoulder throbs painfully, as does my back from the impact. It stuns me for a moment and I hold on for dear life as the ship tilts, I grab the edge of a door as my feet leave the ground. Until the ship rights itself then I crash into the floor, face first.

Refusing to lay down and give up, I push to my feet and make my way as fast as I dare, my legs wide to brace myself in case it banks again. The ship continues to shake and rock making the going hard and treacherous. Using my hand on the wall, I guide myself to the lagoon, hoping that is still where they are. Blood drips on the floor, making me stop and hold out my hand. A drop hits it, and I can feel it now dripping slowly from my head. That can't be good. I reach the door to the lagoon to find it wedged open. With a frown, I slip through, trying to see them. When I don't, I start to panic, they have to be here! They said they wanted to meet here...unless they weren't here yet? If so, where are they now?

"Effie? Auden? Eldon?"

I cry out their names, searching through the darkness, begging whatever god exists to let them be okay. I stumble around the open space, the sand squishing beneath my feet. The siren cuts off leaving me in deafening silence. The red strobe light is the only moving thing, but it barely makes a dent in the shadows in the room. I move to the edge of the water, squinting to make sure. No lights reach this far in here, making the water dark and eerie. The space I used to find sanctuary turning terrifying. Space balls, they aren't here. I will have to keep searching, I can't leave without them.

I turn to leave when I'm flung into the air.

"Gravity filters malfunctioning in the Lagoon." Comes over the speaker.

Time seems to stop as the ship spins wildly, leaving me suspended in mid-air. With a rush, everything speeds up as I land in the water with a splash. Gasping, I kick myself to the surface. I break through with a gasp, drawing in oxygen as fast as I can.

The ship tilts again sending me back below the blue depths. I try to pull myself back up, my arms flapping wildly. Chairs and other objects from the room stream through the water as it rushes around the spinning room. A chair hits me, making me scream underwater as another hits me from behind, spinning me around. I feel something crack as I scream in pain. My body gets hit from every angle.

My lungs scream as I try to figure out what way is up. My eyes dart around, looking for anything to pierce the hazy blue water. Dots start in forming in front of my vision as my body gasps for oxygen. I twist desperately, my legs kicking furiously. A red light flashes and I desperately kick my way to it, using it like a beacon. I try to dodge the debris as the ship stops spinning for a moment and the gravity filters obviously flicker back on.

Breaking the surface of the water with a sputter, I suck down air to my abused lungs. Not wanting to get trapped again, I swim as fast as I can to what used to be the shore. Crawling, I try to get to my feet only to fall at an ache in my ribs. Gritting my teeth, I stumble in the sand as I race for the door, my wet feet sinking, slowing me down as my clothes are heavy on my body.

Sliding through the door, I find myself in a heap against the opposite wall, my chest heaving as water drips to the floor, mixing with my blood, turning it pink. Not one minute later, the door to the lagoon slides shut as an automated warning blares over-head. I look at the window to the lagoon as water steadily rises in the space I just escaped.

"Lagoon compromised. Ship in full failure, please make your way calmly to the nearest shuttle."

Fuck. Pushing myself up, I start towards the shuttles, intent on finding them there. If not, I will go back and search my unit, then Effie's.

"Level G lost. Explosions sensed in level D. Air locks sealed."

Fuck, it sounds like the whole ship is dying. What the hell happened?

In the corridor, an explosion goes off again and I only just manage to stay on my feet as the ship rocks with it. Another comes from behind me, sending me sprawling to the floor, luckily I manage to catch myself on my arms but they give out under the pressure. My ears ring as I pick my head up from the floor littered with glass and metal. I can feel blood running down my cheeks. Looking around in a daze, the words from the warning system blur together. I try to get to all fours, only for my legs to give out. My hands scramble along the floor as I try to pull myself to safety. I can feel my front being cut as I manage to crawl to the corner of the corridor. Using the wall, I pull myself to my feet. Placing my head on the cool wall, I give myself a second to come around. Blowing out a breath, I push away, my feet steadier. I'm turning around when I hear my name screamed. Spinning, I try to see through the dark. I'm back in the corridor at the end of my row of units. Maybe I hit my head harder than I thought and am I hearing things? But no, there it is again...

"INDY!"

"Effie?!" I shout, my voice cutting out with a hacking cough halfway through. I spit blood and water to the floor.

"Indy!" The excited scream comes again, closer this time. I let my abused body rest for a minute as four shapes lumber through the darkness in front of me. The one at the front flings itself at me. I smell Effie before I see her and I lock my arms around her, my back on the wall to steady us.

I offer her a quick hug before letting go. Eldon and Auden stand behind her, looking relieved. Cain pops from in between them and offers me a shit eating grin.

"Couldn't just wait to be rescued could you, speed demon."

Smiling, I go to answer when the speaker sounds again.

"Ship's shuttles fifty percent depleted."

"Fuck, we need to get out of here," I warn. Effie cries but grabs my outstretched hand.

"Eff, where's your dad?" I rush the words out as I yank her down the corridor after me.

"He was at home." She gasps as she stumbles behind me. Okay, that's good, that means he will be at the closest shuttle and he won't leave without his little girl. I pick up the pace, the sound of running feet slapping on the floor the only sound. The ship carries on tilting as we run.

We skid around the corner to the closest shuttle to Effie's unit and I cry in relief when I see the light still blinking next to it. Cain puts me on my feet and I stumble over to it.

I bang on the small window into the shuttle. Howard's relieved face appears before the door slides open.

"Girls!" He cries before surrounding us in his arms. I step back and freeze when I see the people in the shuttle. I count and with each number, my heart speeds up. There are only two empty seats. Unwilling to freak Effie out, I step back, my guys behind me.

"Get in the shuttle Effs." I smile reassuringly at her as she grabs my hand and tries to pull me in after her. Howard's eyes flick behind me before resting on me again. I see the knowledge in his eyes. He knows I won't leave anyone. He knows what that means. He nods, but I see the tears in his eyes. He gently grasps Effie's arm and pulls her into the shuttle.

"Indy?" She turns to me, confused.

"There isn't enough room, babe. You get in this one we will go to the next one." Her eyes widen before she flings herself in my arms, shouting at me. I gently stroke her hair as I swallow my tears.

"It's okay," I whisper as I rock her.

"Get in the shuttle good looking," Eldon says. I let go of Effie and turn to them, defiance in every line of my body.

"No. The more we argue, the less time we have." With that, I turn and push Effie. She stumbles and I step back, the automatic door closing between us. Her faces smashes against the glass as she shouts for her dad to open the door.

"Love you, Effs. I'll see you again." I promise. Ignoring the tears on her face, I press the emergency release next to the door.

"Shuttle launching, please step back." The voice emanates, making her struggle harder.

"Get her in her seat, Howard. Thank you for everything. I love you both." With that, I step back and watch as my best friend is dragged kicking and screaming to her chair. She cries like her heart is breaking as she raggedly screams my name over and over again. I turn away as the shuttle detaches and launches into space.

The guys' stricken faces have the tears flowing harder.

"We need to get to the next shuttle," I dash my arm across my wet cheeks, my focus now on getting us out.

"What's the likelihood of an empty shuttle, good looking?" Eldon crosses his arms.

"You should have gone with her!" Cain warns, his face serious.

"No," I clench my jaw. "I am not leaving you. Get it through your head. Now, we don't have time to waste. We need to get to a shuttle." They nod as fresh determination lights their eyes. The ship rocks again and Auden catches me as I fall.

"Ship will destruct in five minutes." The automated voice warns.

We look at each other before Eldon snatches my hand and pulls me. We sprint down the corridor heading to the next shuttle.

My heart clenches. Shit, Barrott. Surely he will have got out, right? He would have been in the crew quarters, one of the safest areas with the most shuttles. But even as my logic comforts me, my heart screams that he wouldn't have left me, no matter the unresolved issues between us. All that seems so silly right now. What I wouldn't do to have him here.

We arrive at the next shuttle, distracting me from my thoughts. The bay is empty. Eldon screams as he kicks the wall.

"T-minus four minutes to complete destruction."

"Where's the next one?" Auden shouts as I pant. I eye the numbers on the wall and freeze.

"This is the last one."

They all turn to me. I swallow hard.

"This is the last one on this floor." I blink hard and face my guys.

"So, we go to the next floor!" Cain screams. I shake my head sadly.

"They will be gone, they were closest to the dining room."

"What do we do Indy?" Auden looks at me, desperation on his face. Everything slows down as my adrenaline pumps through me, my tutor's words about thinking well under pressure running through my head. I run all possible scenarios and discard those which won't work.

"INDY!" Eldon roars. I snap my head up, a plan forming.

"Our only shot is a flyer. We need to get to the training dock. It's on this floor. I can fly us out, there's enough room for all of us and they won't have been taken as people can't fly them." My back straightens as I speak, my usual courage returning along with a heavy dose of adrenaline which chases away all the pain momentarily and clears my head.

"That's my girl." Cain smiles.

"T-minus three minutes."

Grabbing the closest hand, I turn and sprint, my aim on getting us to the flyers. I can't fail, not this time. I couldn't save my parents, but I will save them.

The corridors blur as we race through the dying ship. My chest is tight and my body is exhausted but still, I go on. I can see the loading bay doors up ahead when the figure pacing in distress before it comes into view. All our arguments and heartache don't matter now. I smile and throw myself at him with a sob, uncaring about the last words we said to each other. If we are going to die, I want to do it with him knowing that I still care.

"Oh god, Indy," Barrott cries as he curls his arms around me. I quickly accept his comfort before pushing away.

"I couldn't find you... I saw the men in your unit but then I didn't know if you had gotten out! I have been searching but I saw the shuttle near yours had gone so, I figured you had left but then it was too late. All the other shuttles were gone, I came here in a panic."

I don't let myself hesitate, I stop him with a quick, determined kiss to his lips before facing the doors.

"We need to get out of here."

He nods, blinking in a daze at me. I grin before jumping out of his arms and using my hand to unlock the doors. They slide open, maddeningly slow, and I squeeze through when they are halfway open, the others doing the same.

I jog across the docks and whoop when I see the flyers still there. I pick the closest biggest one. Reaching the loading zone at the back, I enter my code, the panel sliding up and out to reveal a ramp.

"Get in!" I yell as another explosion rocks us.

"T-minus two minutes."

They run past me. Once they are in, I quickly close the door and make my way through the ship to the cockpit. Once there, I drop into the pilot's seat and strap in. Cain drops into the co-pilot's with a wink at me.

"I'm the best you've got baby, now tell me what to do."

I grin before explaining as I flick on switches. Engaging the engines, igniting the fuel and releasing the clasp to the bay.

"I'm steering. I will programme us to the nearest shuttle and it will follow them down. It will be rough as we are in the blast zone. Keep your hands on that stick and let me know if the sensors in front of you go off."

Not looking to see if he understood, I release the brakes and push the ship into movement. Flipping the last switch, which will open the doors, I wait.

"Come on!" I shout as the warning light for the bay goes off, announcing the doors opening.

"T-minus one minute."

Fuck! Even though the ramp out into space is only part way descended I steer us to it, the flyer smoothly crossing the distance. With a yell, we burst out of the ship and into space. I try to put as much distance between us and it as possible.

Debris and broken ship parts litter the area around us, making me have to manually evade them as the sensors scream at me.

"Cain, flip the switch marked beacon!" I shout while evading a huge, metal ship panelling.

"Done!"

"Okay boys, time to get out of here. Hold on."

I engage the thrusters, pushing us further away. We hurtle through space and away from our dying ship. The shock wave of the ship exploding reaches us and shakes our ship dangerously, parts and pieces flying at the hull.

Opening the screen, I spot the beacon of the shuttles. It looks like they are descending onto a close planet. I lock on, setting the autopilot just in case.

"Warning, engine one damaged."

Spinning to the controls on the left, I see the engine overheating. God help us. I don't bother telling the guys the likelihood of us exploding when we reach the planet's atmosphere. Instead, I focus on trying to prolong it for as long as possible.

The planet appears below us, green and purple swirling as shuttles float down through its atmosphere. The only chance we have is to speed up, to crash instead of land. Steeling myself, I push us harder, the ship burning up as we descend onto the planet. The going is rough as we all hold on for dear life. Eventually, we break through the atmosphere. I don't take time to look at the planet, I locate the first piece of land. I lock in the coordinates, praying to everyone it will be close enough.

"What's going on, are we landing there?" Someone shouts when a strip of green appears before us.

"Well, more like crashing, but yes." I grin as I stop the engines, not wanting to push them too far.

"Indy!"

They scream as we falter mid-air before dropping. At the last second, I grab the controls and slow our descent.

I whoop as the air streams past us; this is so much better than a speeder. I look at Cain as he grins at me.

"Once a speed demon, always a speed demon." He laughs as he rides it out, his trust in me astounding.

"Please keep your legs and arms inside the vehicle as we come to a stop and thank you for flying with Indy Express." I laugh as the ground meets the bottom of the ship, the noise grating on my ears.

We skate over the ground, dirt and debris flying up and hitting the ship. We stop with a sudden smash as the front end of the ship meets the ground. I'm flung forward, my head smashing into the control panels. Something warm drips down my face as it starts to go dark, the flashing of the brakes warning me we are rolling. Before I pass out, I flip the switch to lock us in place. Well, at least we aren't on an exploding ship anymore.

CHAPTER TWELVE

GROUND – DAY ONE

GROANING, I open my eyes. They instantly water, so I slam them shut again. My mouth feels like sawdust and my poor abused head is throbbing. Determined to at least see if my guys are okay, I slowly flicker my eyes open again. Metal ceiling with wires hanging down greets me, only confusing me more. Wasn't I in the cockpit? Heaving myself up, I have to grip onto the bench I'm laying on when the world tilts sideways. Dropping my head between my legs, I breathe through the dizziness and sickness. When I feel somewhat more human, I let my eyes wander around the flyer. I don't see any of the guys and we seem to be powered down. The good news is it seems to be in one piece.

"Indy, shit, you're awake! Come look at this, speed demon." Cain's voice snaps my head around to where I see him grinning, standing at the open ramp. Blood is matted to the left side of his face and his right eye is black but I've never been so pleased to see him.

When I carry on just staring, he starts to get self-conscious and touches his eye before wincing.

"Is-" I have to clear my throat before I can carry on. "Is everyone okay?" He nods, holding his hand out to me.

"Yep, come see."

I drop my palm in his and he gently pulls me to my feet. He

twines our fingers and drops a kiss on my forehead before winking and pulling me out of the flyer after him.

The light blinds me, leaving me squinting into the area we crashed into. Wait, is that the sun? Space balls, I can't remember the last time I felt actual sunlight on my face, I tilt my head back, letting it heat me. Even on Earth, the sun is constantly blocked by the smog and onboard all they had was that fake shit.

"Indy, what the fuck are you doing up and about? You should be resting." Barrott's unmistakable growl has me smiling before I open my eyes to see him. My jaw hangs open when my eyes land on him, erm. Brain malfunction. He's shirtless, showing off an impressive six-pack with one of those delicious V's and a black happy trail leading into his cargo pants. Blindly, I try to drag my gaze to his face, but I just keep staring at his skin - the muscles.

"Indy, you okay?" I hear one of the brothers ask but honestly, I'm contemplating licking Barrott to see if he tastes as good as he looks. Maybe I hit my head harder than I thought.

"Indy." The warning has me dragging my eyes to his, his eyebrow is arched and he looks annoyed, but I can see his lips fighting a smile. Shit, okay. What was the question?

"I'm fine. So, where are we?" I reluctantly pull my eyes away and flick them over the brothers who are standing next to Barrott. They also only seem to have superficial wounds, which is good. Now that I'm not distracted by the beauty that is Barrott, I start to take in the environment around us.

Holy space balls, we definitely aren't on Earth anymore.

Two suns hang in the bright blue and purple sky, one smaller and lower but there none the less. The ground beneath us is squishy and a weird mossy green colour. Mountains span as far as I can see on one side of us. The other side, behind Barrott, is just sky and I frown before slipping around him to see. The front of our flyer is hanging on the edge of a fucking cliff. Well, what I am guessing is a cliff, even if the rock face is pink and purple. Seriously, it looks like Barbie spunked on it.

Grinning at my amazing flying skills, I look out at the foreign world stretched around us. Purple and green mix together below; obviously plant life and trees. Weird noises, which I am guessing are animals, sound out everywhere; the planet buzzing with life. Frowning, I scan the horizon again. I don't see any smoke or beacons of distress. So where is everyone? Turning back to the others, my training kicks in.

"We need to set the beacon in the flyer off. I will do that soon and I'll see how much damage our landing did. I'll try and scan the environment as well and see if it's in any of our databases. We need someone to find supplies, water and food, and check the surrounding area for any dangers or others. Someone needs to set up shelter in and around the flyer since we don't know what time it will get dark. Oh, and I'll try and make contact with whatever is left of Dawnbreaker too... is that everything?" Nibbling on my lower lip, I cock my head when they all stare at me incredulously. Fidgeting, I start to get annoyed.

"What?"

Eldon shakes his head "Good looking, we have been trying to sort out everything since we woke up, but well, we were sort of lost and you wake up and start barking orders and suddenly we know what to do? You are a woman of many talents." He winks before turning to Auden.

"We will search the area for any dangers." He turns to Barrott. "If you can look for water? I'm guessing you have had the most training. Cain can help Indy while setting up camp here. That okay?" Everyone nods and starts to move around now, all filled with determination. Grinning, I watch my men as they work together. Auden and Eldon trot up to me, their jackets thrown over their shoulders.

"Be careful," I warn. "We don't know what's out there, the indigenous life or hostile-" Eldon pecks me on the lips, silencing me, and Auden does the same straight after. My brain malfunctions again - it has happened a lot recently. Honestly, I'm debating the pros and cons of a brother sandwich with me as the meat... or cheese, whatever you fancy. Have I always been this dirty minded? Yes, yes I have.

"Got it, good looking. You worry about saving our asses, okay?"

My brain is still stuck on the idea of brother sandwich - seriously, these guys are going to kill me. By the time I'm back down to whatever this planet is, all I can see of them is their retreating backs as they fade into the wilderness. Barrott steps up next, scowling at where the brothers just were. Before I can second guess myself, I fling myself into his arms. He grunts, but catches me.

"I'm glad you're okay," I whisper into his shoulder. He sighs against me, his arms tightening.

"I was so worried about you Inds. Once everything is less crazy we will talk about what happened. For now, just worry about making contact okay?" I nod into his shoulder, letting his warmth run into me.

"Indy-" He stops before gripping me tighter under the thighs. "I know a lot of stuff has happened recently, just never doubt how I feel about you okay? And that I'm sorry I've been such an idiot. But I can't imagine being here with anyone else." Pulling back, I look at him in confusion.

He gently moves my hair out of my face, his eyes warm and his smile gentle.

"I'll always come for you Inds, whether that's in space or on some backwards planet. We are in this together. Now and forever." Smiling, I go to kiss his cheek, but he moves at the last minute and we both freeze as our lips connect. I can pretend to forget the kiss onboard and blame it on fear and adrenaline, but this one? We are both stock still, our lips barely touching. I don't even breathe, scared he will move away. With a groan, he snaps back into action, gripping the back of my head and brutally kissing my parted lips before dropping me gently to the floor and striding away.

I stand there staring after him in shock, touching my swollen lips. What the hell is going on? Did he hit his head?

"Well, looks like it got interesting. I wondered when he was going to grow some balls." Cain wraps his arms around me from behind as we watch Barrott fade into the distance. Long after he's gone, I kick myself into action. I don't have time to stand here daydreaming.

"Looks like it's me and you," I warn. He laughs before squeezing me and dropping his arms.

"Wouldn't have it any other way, speed demon. Come on, let's save them."

SPACE BALLS, I forgot how much sweating is disgusting. Onboard, your temperature is regulated and I can't remember the last time I properly sweated. Now? It's pouring down me in horrible wet waves.

"Got it, you little bastard." Huffing, I pull myself from below the control panel and stare at it.

"Please baby, work for momma." Crossing my fingers, I input the code and flick on the power. She hums, then starts sputtering.

"No, no, come on." Muttering to myself, I drop back down under the unit and start messing with the wires again until she runs smoothly.

"Yes, baby, that's it!" Grinning, I jump up and start booting up the systems. The screens flick on and light green, showing me it's working. We might not be taking off anytime soon, but we can use the beacon and track whatever is left of Dawnbreaker. Giddy with myself, I start doing my happy dance only to stop when a laugh breaks out behind me. Spinning, I grin at Cain. He's standing with a bag in his hand, obviously just coming in from outside.

"What's wrong, Cain, scared of my moves?" I wink at him. He smirks before dropping the bag and strutting to me. I gulp at the

135

intensity on his face, but don't move away. Expecting him to grind on me, I giggle when he grabs my hand and spins me in a circle. Pulling me back to him, he starts twisting me and twirling me around the little space. I can't seem to stop laughing and the grin is stretched permanently on my face. He pulls me to him again, his arms around me as he watches me. The laughter dies at the look in his eyes.

"I know this whole thing is a shit storm but I'm so glad I'm with you. If I was going to get stranded on an alien planet with anyone..." He trails off, his forehead meeting mine. The world seems to disappear, leaving just us. The worry for the others, the pain in my head, all my fears disappear.

"I had this whole plan for our second first kiss," he murmurs.

"What?" I ask stupidly. He smiles softly, looking between my eyes and my lips.

"I wanted it to be perfect. I didn't want you to regret it this time."

Sucking in a deep breath, I look at his plump pink lips. "What did you imagine?"

"We were under the stars, in our spot. You would be standing before me like an angel, that smile that gets me into trouble on your beautiful face."

"We are under the stars now..." I whisper before pushing everything else away and reaching up on my tiptoes until our lips meet. It starts out slowly, just a pressing of lips, but soon, all the pent-up tension and need bursts through us until we are devouring each other. Fighting each other for control like we always do, it's brutal and perfect. Gripping onto his hair, I push deeper, letting his tongue tangle with mine as his hands cup my ass, pulling me to him, until there is no space between our bodies. I can feel him hardening and it only drives me wilder, everything coming out in the kiss as I pull back to nip on his lip. He groans, and I pull away to suck in a breath. His lips never leave my skin, trailing from my cheek to my neck as I try to remember how to breathe. I know the others could be back at any moment, I know I need to be concentrating on the beacon, but with Cain right in front of me telling me he planned our kiss? The ever cocky upper letting me see inside again, how can I say no?

Pushing my hands under his shirt, I trail them along his muscles, my fingers grazing his lines as he nips and licks down my neck. With a groan, I tip my head to the side, letting him have better access. He lifts his head slowly, his eyes blazing. We stare at each other, breathing heavily, before he slams his lips back to mine.

I hear a beep go off behind me but I ignore it, stretching to grab his hair and yank him to me. It goes off again, and in the back of my muddled mind, something is screaming that it's important. Before I can latch onto the thought, he's kissing me again, wiping away all rational thinking. When it comes again, I pull back reluctantly. Cain goes to speak but I put my finger to his swollen lips.

"What-"

"Shush!"

Waiting, I tilt my head. It slowly comes again and I spin. There, on the screen behind me, is the signal from the Dawnbreaker, the comms unit in the flyer latching onto it.

"Holy shit!"

"What?" He asks confused, his hands caressing my sides as he pushes up against my back.

"It survived."

CHAPTER THIRTEEN

GROUND – DAY ONE

SPINNING, I grab his cheeks and plant one on him before hurrying to the control panel.

Hitting the voice activation and onboard computer I wait.

"Identify."

"Indy Stewart," I say, bouncing on my toes.

"Welcome, Indy."

"Computer, bring up coordinates for Dawnbreaker. Search for any escape pods or flyers from on board and map their locations."

"One moment."

That moment seems to take forever, as Cain and I anxiously wait. Eventually, on the black screen in front of me, green dots start to appear, as does basic terrain information. Something in me loosens knowing we aren't the only ones here. Now all I –we - need to do is find Effie and Howard and get to whatever is left of the Dawnbreaker.

"Okay, it looks like there's a large crash site not too far from here, it's the closest one so we should start by going there first." I murmur while looking at the map. Cain drops his head on top of mine and watches as I look through the terrain and other crash sites.

"Damn, we are really spread out."

"Indy?" Barrott shouts, smiling I jump up and make my way outside, Cain hot on my heels. My smile disappears when I see him. He looks exhausted and his shirt is shredded with blood welling from cuts on his chest. Spinning, I run back into the flyer and grab the emergency med bag stored in the back. Hurrying outside, I jog to where he is slumped on the ground, a grimace on his face. I fall to my knees in front of him, worrying on my bottom lip.

"What happened?" I ask as softly I grab his shirt, and he helps me pull it off with a grunt.

"Something pushed me down a hill." Blinking repeatedly, I stare at him stupidly.

"Something as in natural wildlife?" Chastising myself, I pull out the wipes and start on the cuts on his chest, trying to ignore his warm skin and muscles that contract.

"Maybe."

Looking up, panic claws through me.

"But you don't think so?" I say slowly.

He sighs. "No."

Shit, so either someone made it all the way here from the crash sites, depending on where it was or there is someone or a lot of someone else's out there. Alien life? I mean I always wondered, but our government told us our section of the galaxy was empty. Done with cleaning the cuts, I grab the sealer tube and spray it on them, it closes the slashes quickly until all that's left is a pink mark. Sitting back on my heels, I go to speak when a grunt sounds from behind me. Turning my head, I spy Eldon and Auden lugging a metal box between them.

"You okay for a minute?" Waiting until Barrott nods, I jump up and walk to the brothers.

"I know good looking, we rule," Auden says with a wink. He drops his half and opens his arms for me. Rolling my eyes as Eldon swears as he struggles with his end, I walk into the hug. Auden lifts me off my feet and spins me around. Squealing, I hold on, laughing when he puts me down. I manage to turn in his arms and face Eldon.

"What did you find?" My mind instantly reverts back to our lack of supplies, the shuttle will have a few, but not a lot.

"Food, water and some other stuff we can't identify." I nod and go to look when he carries on. "And that's not all." He looks around and turns to me, grimly.

"We found the Dawnbreaker, well half of it."

WE DECIDE to make a plan instead of running off half-cocked. I make sure everyone has something to eat and drink and we pack up everything we will need. I spend a few minutes memorising the map of the other crash sites and checking the flyer over. Then I power it down and lock it from the outside.

With one last look back, we set off into the forest, the mood somber. If the Dawnbreaker is gone, what are we going to do? How will we reach Ayama? How many people survived the crash?

Questions pepper my mind, but there is nothing I can do about them now. I need to concentrate on one thing at a time. The main one, surviving down here.

We head in the direction Auden and Eldon pointed out with Barrott in the lead and the brothers behind him. Cain and me, watching our backs. After all, we can't be too careful if something is out here. I wonder what attacked Barrott.

At first, the forest we are trudging through looks similar to that of the ones that used to grow on Earth, but the further in we go, the more the differences become obvious. The trees aren't just green and brown, but pink and purple ones start to crop up. Great big ones that create canopies over us as they twist together. The ground turns from the grass-like consistency to multi-coloured flowers which move and twist like animals. There are animal noises, but they are more brutal, louder. No sweet bird songs. The heat starts to increase as well, until sweat drips down me in steady waves, the humidity finally affecting me. Despite it all, it's beautiful, in an alien sort of way.

The air smells clean and fresh, unlike the last time I was on our planet. The plants and wildlife are alive and thriving, not like our dead world. There's no comms units and technology placed every two meters, with tall skyscrapers built in place of nature. There's something so fresh and new about this place. The animals don't seem to be hunted into extinction and the trees cut for things we don't need.

"Let's take a five-minute break," Barrott calls as he stops in a small clearing, the trees making a circle around us. Nodding, I drop my pack and stretch out my sore muscles. Finished with my stretches, I look up to see they are all staring at me. When I raise my eyebrow. they all scatter. Barrott coughs and turns to dig in his pack, Auden and Eldon wink before slumping on the ground, their backs to a tree. Cain grins but turns to look out into the forest.

"I'm going to pee, I'll be back in a minute."

"I'll go with you," Barrott says while turning to face me, a stern expression on his face. Groaning, I don't bother fighting him, knowing he'd probably just stalk me anyway. I don't go far, just past a couple of trees.

"Okay, wait here," I warn Barrott, and ignoring his grumbling, I round the tree and pull down my trousers. They stick to me in an unattractive way making me cringe. Squatting, I do my business and pull my trousers back up. I'm just doing the button when something darts between the trees in front of me. Warily, I look around as I wait for it to move again, instead, it slinks out from the shadowed area.

It looks like a black panther, but it has white markings swirling over its fur and it's double the size. What looks like a large tail swishes behind it, but instead of a single tail, it branches into two separate sections about half way down its length.

"Er,, Barrott?" I call, my voice seems to startle it because it trots closer then drops to its butt in front of me, a forked tongue lolling out.

"Aren't you a cutie?" I purr at it. It yawns, showing me it's large teeth, two massive fangs hanging over its lips.

"Okay, so a bit scary too," I choke out.

Barrott comes skidding around the tree only to stop cold when he spots the big cat.

"Okay, move slowly Inds." He keeps his voice low and holds his hand out to me. The cat's ears go back at his voice and it stands. I slowly put my palm in Barrott's and start to inch away. Before I can flinch, it growls and flings itself in front of me, standing before me, growling at Barrott.

"Okay. Erm, I think it's trying to protect me?" I ask, freezing in case it decides to turn and take a chunk out of me.

"Fucking shit, only you could pick up a stray on an alien planet!" he yells, throwing his hands in the air.

I cross my arms at his tone. "It's not like I sat peeing wishing a large freaking cat would come out to be my friend," I gripe, only to trail off when it turns to me. It purrs and rubs his head on me, the force knocking me to the ground. From here, it's bigger than me. It drops on me and starts rubbing itself all over me, still purring. Loud enough to shake the ground. Blinking, I stare at Barrott.

"Nice kitty?" I squeeze out, my chest hurting from the weight of it. It's head swings to me and his tongue slithers out again as I narrow my eyes.

"No, don't you dare," I warn. I swear it grins at me before it swipes its tongue across my cheek. Swearing, I try to wipe away the saliva.

"Bad alien kitty, no, stop!" I yell as it starts to lick my face again.

"God damn it, stop!" I shout. It blows a breath in my face and goes back to rubbing itself on me. Laughter has my head snapping up. Cain, Eldon, and Auden must have come while I was trying to fight off the slobber machine. Cain is bent over the tree laughing as Eldon and Auden grin at me.

"A little help?" I ask grumpily.

"Nope, that's all you speed demon," Cain says between laughs.

"I peed on that tree, so jokes on you." I laugh when he wrinkles his nose at me, his laughter cutting off. Barrott chokes out a laugh at that and shakes his head at me.

"Okay play times over, say goodbye to your friend Inds."

Oh yeah, like I can just shoo it away? Fucking idiots just stand around watching. I'm going to get back at them for this.

"Okay kitty, time to go," I coo. It stops purring and watches me.

"Come on, get up," I ask nicely. It blows air in my face again.

"No. Up," I warn, pointing at the ground next to me. It watches me, not moving.

"Off now." I harden my voice and narrow my eyes. Its ears drop as it slinks off me, laying next to me making a pitiful whining noise. Groaning, I stand up.

"Alright, alright. I'm sorry, that was mean. But you were heavy," I moan as I hesitantly pat its head. It starts purring automatically and jumps up to stand in front of me.

"Okkkay. Bye." I shake my head at the weirdness and turn to the guys. I pick my way over to them when Eldon smiles at me.

"Looks like you have another stalker," he says pointing behind me, turning I see the giant cat is right behind me, making me jump and let out a girly scream.

"Oh great just what I need, as if Barrott isn't enough," I moan, gripping my chest from the scare.

"Shit, Indy look at me!" Barrott shouts. I do, confused.

He rushes forward and grips my face, turning it from side to side. "Do you three idiots see this?" he asks in awe. I start to panic as they all crowd around me.

"See what? Tell me what the hell is happening?" My voice is high pitched, but damn it all to space and back, it's my face!

"Holy..."

"How?"

"WHAT?" I screech.

"Erm, I think your stalker might have healed your face." Cain offers.

"What?" I ask dumbly.

"When it licked you. It must have something in its saliva which promotes healing. Your cuts are healing and your bruising has disappeared altogether," Barrott says reassuringly like that's an everyday occurrence. I try not to freak out, but I must not do a very good job.

"It's a good thing Inds," he says softly. I nod, my eyes wide.

"Sure," I squeak out, making them all laugh. He drops his hands and steps back. I look at the cat as it lets out a purr.

"Erm, thank you I guess?"

Space balls, I am talking to a cat now. It stretches and trots to my side with a huff. Breathing deeply, I try to swallow my panic. When I am sort of under control, I turn back to the guys.

"Okay, I think we should start walking again."

They nod and I follow them back through the trees, my new cat best friend behind me.

CHAPTER FOURTEEN

Ground – Day One

WE START WALKING AGAIN, pointedly ignoring the giant cat stalking me. When it does no more than follow, I start to relax. The trees pass us in a blur as I concentrate on putting one foot in front of the other and not falling over.

I don't know what the cat did to me, but even my headache disappears. In fact, I feel better than I have for a while. We carry on, trudging through the alien forest. Sweat continues to pour off me, and my breathing becomes laboured. I stop mid-step at the sound of running water. We all share a look and Barrott pushes ahead faster, a new determination in his steps. We break through the trees into what looks like a dream.

A huge waterfall stands in the corner of a clearing, nestled between two cliff edges. A pool of clear water stands at the bottom of it. The water lapping at the stones surrounds the edges. Flowers in all colours are peeking out from rocks, stones and even the cliff. Trees offer shade on the outside but the middle is filled with sun, the water gleaming bright. Ignoring the others, I step into the clearing, stopping just short of the water.

I'm in awe, the water is so clear that you can see the stones underneath, resting at the bottom. I hesitantly bend over and dip my finger in, the cold has me moaning in ecstasy. I search the water for any signs of anything harmful or dangerous. When a splash sounds, I blink and watch as my cat stalker paddles around before looking at me and huffing.

Is he laughing at me? Bloody cat. I grin as I stand back up.

I grab the bottom of my top and yank it up, leaving it on the stones. Bending over, I pull my boots off next, then my socks. I'm just unbuttoning my jeans when I hear a cough behind me. Looking over my shoulder, I see Barrott glaring at me as Cain smirks. The brothers smile, but their cheeks are flushed. I grin impishly and drop my trousers making Barrott swear.

"Indy, don't you dare!" he warns, but it's too late. I wade into the water, moaning in bliss as it cools my overheated skin. I dip my head back, letting my hair get wet and shut my eyes as the water laps at my face. A splash next to me has me lifting my head and opening my eyes as the cat flicks water at me.

I glare at it, before splashing it back. It turns, its tails flicking more water at me as it paddles to the edge before getting out and stretching out on the stone bank in the sun. Shaking my head, I look back at my men. Eldon and Auden are stripping down, but Cain and Barrott are both watching me.

"Come on, it's so nice in here. Don't be a pussy!" I shout before dunking under and swimming up to the fall. The water feels amazing and I pop back up just short of the falls and turn my back to it. Eldon and Auden are swimming over to me as Cain strips off. Barrott is glaring, his arms crossed as he watches us from the shore.

Grinning, I duck under the water and swim to the shore. When I get there, I bolt out of the water and fling myself at him. He catches me automatically as I wrap myself around him.

"Indy," he growls.

I smile sweetly at him. "Come and swim with me."

"No." He narrows his eyes.

"What if there is something in the water you need to protect me from?" I ask. He thinks it through before sighing loudly.

"Fine. Bloody woman," he moans as I jump off him and wait.

He pulls off his shirt, and quickly shucks off his boots and trousers. I try not to stare, I really do. Cold water showers me from behind, making me realise I had just been gawking. Smiling in embarrassment, I jump back in the cold water and swim to Cain who is laughing at me. I stick my tongue out at him on the way past and carry on to the brothers.

"Who's going to dive under and see what's behind there?" I ask them, treading water.

We look at each other before all diving under the water. I swim underneath the waterfall and break the surface on the other side. Eldon pops up to my left and Auden to my right. Grinning, I pull myself up on the rock ledge. The rock is black and smooth, with white glints speckled everywhere, breaking up some of the shadows from the waterfall. I glance over my shoulder to see the water; you can't see through to the other side. The ledge runs around the rock, a curved wall hidden back here. Turning back, I see the brothers watching me. I smile before sitting, my feet dangling in the water.

"You both okay?" I ask.

It's been so crazy since we crashed, I don't think I have asked. I have even ignored my own feelings, trying to concentrate on keeping us alive. Eldon climbs up next to me as Auden swims towards me. He braces his arms on my thighs and treads water, floating between my legs.

"We are fine. You going to talk to us about what happened with…" He trails off, looking embarrassed. I cup his cheek.

"I'm okay, luckily the ship exploded just in time," I joke. It falls flat and I sigh. "Honestly, I was scared. But he didn't get any further than roughing me up a little."

"We are so sorry, good looking. I never thought he would go that far. We would have never have left you alone if-" Eldon cuts out, both of their eyes are filled with unshed tears and filled with shame.

"Look, what's done is done. It was a crazy day, with them rebel freaks kidnapping me, and your father, then the explosion…" It's my turn to trail of at their shocked looks.

"Kidnapping?" They both say in unison.

I quickly run them through everything that happened. By the end, they both look angry on my behalf and if we were still on board, I would be scared of what they would do.

"I wonder what they did to bring the ship down?" I ponder; it's been bugging me. They obviously knew the brothers' father wouldn't be caught, which means they either planned this or they planned to kill us? But surely they didn't mean to bring the ship down? Did they? If so, why did they approach me about needing my help? Auden sighs before dropping his chin onto my thighs with his arms.

"I guess we'll never know. I'm just glad we had you there."

"He's right, good looking. Without you, we would have all been screwed."

I look away, uncomfortable with their praise. It goes quiet as I think about everything that has happened, letting Effie go, almost dying… their father. His face distorted with anger and lust pops in my head, making me shiver. I see the brothers share a look before they both turn back to me.

"For some reason, I was feeling a little off today. But when you came along, you definitely turned me on." Auden wiggles his eyebrows as he talks.

"I was wondering if you had an extra heart. Mine was just stolen," Eldon adds, making all my fear and stress fade away. I know it isn't healthy to bottle it all up, but right now I don't have the time to be weak. We need to survive and find others, and me curling into a ball and crying isn't going to help. So, I laugh at their cheesy pick-up lines. Eldon smiles at me before kissing my shoulder. Auden drops a kiss on my hand and it's like everything is okay again. With so much changing, it's nice to see some things staying the same.

"Come on, we better get back before Barrott freaks." I slide back into the water and dunk under.

We all spend the next hour or so splashing and swimming before Barrott announces it's time to leave. He even sounds sad. We slip out of the water and get dressed. I catch them throwing me lingering looks, but I don't mention it. Barrott smiles at me before he heads back into the trees.

Looking back sadly at our spot, I turn and follow the others as we set off in our search once again. The water is a beautiful distraction, among such a deadly world. I watch as the trees swallow it up, like our little secret.

WE WALK for another couple of hours, my cat stalker leaping from trees above us. The first time I saw him do it, I screamed but I have got used to it now, even if I do keep a close eye on him. The trees around us start to thin out and Barrott stops, sucking in a breath.

"What?" I huff, exhaustion creeping in. I stop next to him when I see what he stopped for. There, in a crater, is half of the Dawn-breaker. Trees are broken beneath it, and fires are here and there, but the giant ship is laying in the forest in front of us. Although Auden and Eldon told me, seeing it is different. Hopelessness flutters in my chest, as does panic. How will we ever get back? Earth is years away, as is Ayama. We are stuck on an alien planet with no way off.

"What are we going to do?" I ask quietly. I don't know what Barrott hears in my voice but he turns to me, cupping my cheek.

"We survive, one day at a time. Right now we are going to go down there and see if there are any survivors or anything we can use. Then we will decide what to do. Whatever we do, we do together. All of us."

I nod, at least I have them. A head knocks into my side, making me fall into Barrott as the giant cat stalker nudges me, it's weirdly comforting. But I throw it a glare. Pulling myself back to together, I nod again and face the ship. Seeing the devastation brings home just how lucky we were, and how much the rebellion messed up.

"I wonder why they did it?" I ask, staring at the carnage below.

"Who knows," Eldon says.

I look over my shoulder and spot Cain looking at me, something in his eyes has me frowning, but he quickly clears it with a smile. I turn back to the ship and take a deep breath.

"Okay boys, let's go."

Barrott smiles at me, pride shining in his eyes before twining his hand with mine. Grinning at him, I let him lead me down the hill.

CHAPTER FIFTEEN

GROUND – DAY ONE

WHEN WE GET to the bottom of the hill, we all stop with the huge ship in front of us, unsure of where to start.

"Okay, we go about this carefully," Barrott orders. I nod and follow him as he starts to pick his way through the wreckage.

We spend hours combing over the outside of the ship for anyone alive or anything we can use before we find a hole that allows us into the ship. Luckily, it's the top half of the ship, which means we should be able to access the beacon or recording systems at least. If they are intact.

We pick our way carefully through broken hallways, with wires and holes everywhere. Because the ship crashed on its side, we have to move slowly around everything that has fallen. I nearly fall once but Barrott has a tight grip on my arm and pulls me along after him.

"We should check for anything we can use while we are here," Barrott orders. I swallow as I look around at all the doors, knowing what I will find behind at least some.

I hold onto Barrott's hand as we approach a partially open door. The top right-hand side is missing, the edges rough and burnt black. He slips through and manages to unwedge it from the other side, so it slides open.

I help him search the unit, trying to ignore all the personal possessions, knowing the people who lived here are probably dead. I feel horrible about taking their things, unclean almost, but if we are to survive down here we need them.

We search the next three rooms with no issue but when I slip through the fourth door, I freeze. Laid on the floor, face down, is a man. His left arm is missing and blood covers his head but I can see his unseeing eyes from where his head is turned.

Blowing out a breath, I grab a blanket and cover him, it's the best I can offer at the moment. Hopefully, when there are more of us, or when we know what is going on we can come back and bury him and anyone else we find. Making my way up the mangled stairs, I start to search the first bedroom.

The bed is messed like someone was still in it when the siren went off. Drawings cover one of the walls and there are girly decorations pinned here and there. Moving around the bed, I slide the drawer under the bed out and my heart speeds up at the teddy bear laying inside.

Picking it up gently, I hold the stuffed animal. I wonder what happened to the person it belonged to. Sighing, knowing Barrott will be in any minute, I gently put it back and close the drawer. Still crouched, I move over to the storage unit next to the bed.

A sob hiccups out of me when I see the body behind it. I cover my mouth in horror, as tears fill my eyes. There, laid on her side, like she is sleeping, is a little girl. She must be no older than six or seven, with a thick brown afro, dressed in a pink tutu and shimmery top.

A metal fragment pierces her little chest, with blood around the area. God, she must have been so scared. All on her own as she died? My heart almost freezes in my chest at the thought. She must have been so scared, no one should face death alone never mind a child. The tears trickle down my face as I lean forward and close her eyes, unwilling to looking into their empty terrified depths any longer.

"Indy?"

"We have to bury her," I choke out. It's the least she deserves. I can't think clearly, but it seems important that she be buried. Not just left to rot in this tomb-like ship, her bear in the drawer. Barrott crouches next to me, his eyes stricken as he looks at her.

"We will come back. I promise it, Indy. For now, we need to get to control and see if any tracking or beacons work, so we don't end up like them." His voice is strong, but I can see the sadness in his eyes, and he won't look at her again.

I don't bother hiding my tears as I stare at him, needing my strong shadow, needing his strength.

"What happened, Barrott? How did it all go so wrong?"

He sighs and sits on the floor, his back to the bed. His arms open and with a little sob, I land in his lap, burying my head on his shoulder, my eyes still on the little girl.

"I don't know, baby. I have an idea, but it doesn't matter at the minute. All that matters is that we are alive, we are okay. We need to keep moving. I know it's hard, but I need you to be the Indy I know you can be."

I nod and he cups my cheek, making me face him. His hands bracket my face, holding me there as if he knows my eyes want to draw back to the little girl.

"I love that you care so deeply, I do. But I need you. I need that crazy woman who climbs into a flyer as a ship is exploding, who races for fun. I need you to help me save us. I can't do it without you Inds." The desperation in his voice undoes me.

I nod, his words drying my tears up. I can mourn our dead later, for now, I need to concentrate on the living. I just hope to whatever god exists out there, that the people who did this pay.

"Okay," I whisper.

"Come on baby, we can do this." He puts his forehead to mine, almost mirroring how we were the last time we were alone together, before that fight.

"Barrott, were you really going to walk away from me?"

I know it's stupid with everything going on, but I need to know. He takes a deep breath but doesn't hesitate with his words.

Some time between walking away from me and crashing on this alien planet, he seems to have given up on acting proper and keeping his distance.

"No. I don't think I could even if I wanted to. I was jealous and stupid, Inds. I nearly died without telling you how I feel. It would have been my biggest regret, not having you, not loving you. You're my life, Indy Stewart, my family, my everything and I was a fool. I just hope I am not too late. I love you. Always have and always will. Until the stars don't shine anymore, and the sun doesn't rise, my heart beats for you."

My heart races, happiness like never before bursting to life in my chest. The world might be falling apart around us, but if that's what it takes for him to finally admit how he feels... I hate it all a little less.

"You're okay, I guess," I say and bite my lip to hold in my smile.

He groans, closing his eyes as if in pain, and I giggle.

"Pikachu, I choose you?" I try again, uncomfortable with trying to articulate how I feel. He glares at me, and I let the giggle go and try to be serious.

"I love you too, you big idiot. I don't know what I would do without you, I was so scared you were going to leave me," I whisper.

"I know, I regretted those words as soon as I had said them." His eyes search mine, trying to make me feel the truth in his words.

I close my eyes in pain, already wishing I could change how I feel.

"Baby?"

"I love you, I do. But it doesn't change how I feel about the others. I can't help it, I need them. It's crazy and even I can't wrap my mind around it but..."

"Indy."

I stop talking at his growl and look back into his eyes, hoping he won't crush my heart. I wouldn't blame him if he did, what I'm saying is crazy.

"If it takes accepting those idiots to have you, then I will. Maybe if I had made my move earlier, I wouldn't have to, but I can't moan. I understand how easy it is to fall for you." His left hand strokes my cheek gently as he holds me.

My guilt is still riding me, as is the fear of losing him after only just getting him back. I wish I could say I will just walk away from the others, but my heart rebels at the idea.

"What are you saying?" I demand, wanting to be very clear.

"I'm saying we don't have the luxury of second guesses or petty jealousies. Not now. We need to work together to survive. I'm not promising you it will be easy. I will probably get jealous and punch someone, or flip out. But I will try. We are going to need each other to survive this planet," he growls out most of it. like it pains him, but I know Barrott's word is his law.

I don't hesitate now, I lean forward and press my lips to his. He grips the back of my hair, pulling enough to cause me to groan as he plunders my mouth. All the waiting, all the wondering has led to this moment. Being in his arms, admitting everything. It couldn't be any more perfect. He pulls away, and I try to chase him.

"We should get back before they start to look for us," he whispers. I'm happy to see his breathing heavy and his eyes slightly unfocused. Nodding sadly, I plant a quick kiss on his lips and stand up. As he leads me out of the bedroom, I look back at the little girl with a silent promise to not forget her, to come back and put her to rest. I promise her she won't be alone anymore.

WE SEARCH THE OTHER UNITS, my heart breaking at each body until anger starts to burn in me for their pointless deaths. I vow to find out the truth of what happened.

We have to make a few trips outside with our supplies until we have quite the little pile. Filled with sleeping bags, blankets, pillows, food, clothes and more. When we finish our search, we set our sights on getting to Control.

It takes us ages to get to the door of flight control. Having to pass through burnt out hallways, gaps in the floor and closed barriers. The door stands shut, the only thing in the hallway that does. Of course, this wouldn't be easy.

"How do we get in?" I ask, there's no power to the door scanner so I can't hack it, and it's not like we have permission to enter control.

"Move, Inds," Barrott grunts, turning, I blink as he and Cain have fashioned a battering ram. Cain grins as I slip back next to the brothers.

It takes them over twenty tries, with the brothers switching out to help before the door smashes inwards. Barrott slips past the mangled mess then holds his hand out for me. I grab it, and he hauls me safely through, I offer him a smile before turning back to the room.

I'm betting when it was functional it was amazing, it's every pilot's dream to be in here. I just never thought it would be like this. Where screens covered the whole curved front point, they now lay smashed on the floor. Lights hang down, with parts of the ceiling caved in. The comms and audio scanner desk is sparking, with the chairs lying broken on the sides. The captain's chair is burnt and the spinning level it sits on is broken and damaged. The two lower pilot's seats are intact but the computers and screens look damaged.

Tracking, weapons, and security to the right is a mess. The glass table and holo screen have a body laid over it. The cage where weapons used to sit is empty and the gate is hanging down. Overall, it looks like a nightmare, not the fresh new shiny control centre I saw on the introduction to pilots training. I lower my eyes when I see the dead crew members, the blood and gore making me freeze for a moment. The chances of me knowing anyone up here is higher than the level we searched, it makes me hesitant once again. Something I am not used to being.

"You okay?" Cain asks, rubbing my back.

Nodding, I hurry to the control panel on the left, where the second pilot would have sat. I flick on the system and almost cry when it doesn't work, surely it's got to. The flight centre is the most protected place in the whole ship with power being rerouted here in the case of an emergency. Frowning, I shimmy down under the control panel and check the wires, fusing a couple that have snapped. I pick my way through, meticulously checking for any issues. When I find no more, I crawl back out and try again.

The screen flashes before going dark. Damn it. Sticking my hand back under I find one of the wires broken again. Using my hand to hold it together, I press the screen. It lights up this time, some of the pixels broken but still useable.

I quickly turn on tracking and beacon mode, so that other ships in the area can find us and navigate back onto the home page. Frowning at the flashing icon, I press it. I can hear the others murmuring as they work around the room but I focus on my task. I scroll through the communication with Earth log, trying to hold in my shock and horror at the scale of the rebels' attacks. How could they keep this from us? One was sent as we crashed, and there is a half finished one waiting on the screen.

TRANSMISSION LOG 00310
DATE: 2032
MISSION: 43, COLONY
SHIP: DAWNBREAKER
DESTINATION: AYAMA

>.............. Accepted
> The attack was an inside job. Someone high up
has been aiding the rebels, they had access to
our weapons and controls. Only ten people have
the access codes. Do not trust Ha-

THE MESSAGE CUTS OUT, a blood smear marring the screen as if they typed it as they were dying. As a warning.

I quickly click on the message which was sent, trying to ignore the panic the other created. When I realise what I'm seeing, I almost jump for joy.

"Guys!"

"What happened?"

"You okay, speed demon?"

"Tell me you're not hurt."

"Shh, and come here will you!" They all crowd around me, their heat seeping into me and distracting me. Shaking my head, I flick back over the message, checking I'm right.

"They got a distress message out as we were going down. Earth and Ayama know where we are!"

The voices blend together as they all celebrate. I turn, letting the wire go and the screen dies as Auden whoops and picks me up, spinning me around. A bang goes off, making him cover me and we all shut up and throw each other a look.

"We don't know what the stability of the ship is like, we should leave," Eldon says seriously, none of us fights him and we slowly make our way out of the skeleton of the ship. When I get outside, I almost laugh as my cat stalker sits wagging its tail at me.

"It's getting dark, we are better setting up camp here and waiting to see if anyone else comes," I offer, looking around as the sun gets lower, the light barely breaking through the trees. The guys nod and we all start to work together to get a camp together.

I help Cain as we clear a space to sleep, far enough away from the ship in case anything more explodes or falls, but close enough to see if anyone else comes wandering in. Auden and Eldon sort out beds and food, using the things we salvaged from our flyer and some things we managed to find in the ship.

Barrott goes and collects things to start a fire while scouting the area for any predators or issues. My cat stalker stays with me the whole time, watching us curiously.

As the sun finally sets, a cold wind sets in, making me shiver in my shirt. How can a planet be so warm during the day but so cold at night?

Barrott starts a fire and soon we are all sitting around it, munching away on the food we found. The alien stars shine down on us, a large blood red moon lighting up the sky. It casts an eerie glow on the forest and our camp, but beautiful in a unique way.

"You have got to admit, it's a beautiful planet," I say as I lean back on my arms, my feet aimed at the fire.

"Yes, the colours here are amazing," Cain says, looking around. I smile and lean back, looking into the sky.

"I never thought I'd miss space," I say watching the stars twinkle against the sky.

"I wonder how long it will be until someone comes for us?" One of the brothers asks.

"It depends on how quickly they receive the transmissions. The next colony mission is not set to leave for another six months. Ayama is unlikely to send anyone, concentrating on curating the new world there," Barrott says, making the mood turn sombre as well all think of the implications. It means realistically we are trapped on this planet for the foreseeable future.

Sighing, I get to my feet and dust the dirt off my pants.

"Where are you going?" Barrott asks, his eyes narrowed.

"To pee, if that is okay?" I roll my eyes and Cain heaves himself to his feet.

"I'll go with her," he offers.

159

Barrott nods, but keeps his glare on me. I stick out my tongue and his lips twitch.

Cain grabs a torch and follows me as I slowly work my way around our little camp and into the trees. I hesitate at the tree line but my bladder reminds me if I don't pee soon, I might explode. Slipping into the darkened trees, I let Cain's hand on my back warm me.

"I can't remember the last time I was in the wild," he murmurs.

"Me either, it's just so different from Earth."

"Did you see the size of the trees or that creepy flower that moved? I wonder if Ayama is like that?" he asks, shining the light around when we come to three clusters of trees.

"Probably not," I mutter, my thoughts on the rebel's words.

"What do you mean?" he asks as I turn to face him, the torch shining bright between us.

"I- nothing."

He tilts my head up with his finger. "Speed demon?"

I search his eyes before sighing. "Ayama is dying."

The words settle into the space between us and I frown watching him, he looks shocked but it looks forced and his eyes are tight.

"Cain?" I ask suspiciously, stepping away from him.

He licks his lips and looks away from me into the forest. "Better pee so we can get back," he says coldly.

"That's all you have to say when I tell you the planet we are heading for is dying?" I ask incredulously, looking at him like he's a stranger.

"Drop it, Indy." He crosses his arms, still not looking at me.

"You knew?" I accuse, the rebels' words about trusting the wrong people coming back to me. How would he know, unless he is one of them?

A twig breaking has us both turning. Cain rushes to my side and shines the light into the forest searching for the noise.

"Probably just an animal, hurry up so we can get back." He doesn't look at me as he speaks.

I turn away from him and quickly pee before joining him again. We don't speak on our way back to camp, and he feels like someone completely different to me. How could the Cain I thought I knew be part of the rebels? Part of something which killed people, and crashed us on this planet? It just doesn't make sense. The image of that little girl I found flashes in my mind, making me angry again. If he was part of it, I will never forgive him.

When we get back to the camp, I sit next to the brothers and he sits next to Barrott, the atmosphere feels strained and if the looks we are being thrown are anything to go by the others feel it. We all finish eating and pack everything away, sitting and enjoying the silence. Or in my case, trying to figure out how Cain could have been involved.

"Be back in a moment, I need to take a leak," Cain says. He drops a kiss on my head on the way past. I don't smile like I usually would, still concerned about our conversation from before. I catch Barrott's eyes and look away, afraid he can see everything I am trying to hide. I don't want to tell him, he will go after Cain and I could be wrong.

"Alright let's get some rest guys," Barrott says before sliding across and sitting next to me, looking out into the forest, obviously planning on keeping watch.

Nodding, I curl up in the emergency sleeping bag, close enough to the fire for it to warm me and far enough away not to be burnt. My eyes slide shut happily, the day's exhaustion setting in.

I am just sliding into sleep when I hear a grunt and then a bang from the forest. Sitting bolt upright, I watch as Barrott stands and puts his finger to his lips. I nod and wait. The brothers tense next to me. Looking around, I realise Cain isn't back yet.

"Stay here," Barrott whispers before striding off, blending into the shadows of the trees.

"Where's Cain?" I whisper. I look at the brothers who both look worried. They slide out of their sleeping bags and sit on either side of me, wrapping an arm around me for comfort. When minutes pass, I start to get worried about them both.

"They should be back by now!" I murmur, looking around in case they materialize out of thin air. Eldon sighs before standing up, my side instantly cooling without his body heat.

"Stay here, Indy, okay?" he says grabbing a torch and checking to see that it works.

I grab his arm. "It's not a smart plan to go towards the noise and where the other people have disappeared!"

"We need to know if they are okay. Look, your stalker's back. Just stay here with him and we will be back before you know it good looking." He swoops in and kisses my cheek. Auden does the same to the other cheek before standing and nodding at his brother. They throw me one more look before they to blend into the trees.

My cat stalker stretches out in front of me and I nervously pet him waiting for any little noise or movement. Those idiots better be okay, or I am going to kick their ass. The seconds seem to drag by, every little noise making me look around wildly. When the seconds turn into minutes, I start to really panic. Something attacked Barrott earlier and we are on a strange planet where anything could be lurking in the dark. They could be hurt right now, needing me to help. Standing, I look around as if they will magically appear. I grab the last torch and flick it on. I step outside the ring of our sleeping bags and shine it around the camp.

"Barrott? Auden? Eldon? Cain?" Shouting, I lift the torch higher, shining it into the dense forest surrounding our camp.

"Where the hell are you guys?"

I will not panic, I will not panic.

Trees rustle behind me, making me swing around. Stepping back closer to the fire I squint into the darkness. A silhouette against the trees has me gasping. At least eight feet tall, the shape looks human enough but I don't know any human that tall. When it steps out into the light, my jaw drops.

A freaking alien. It's a fucking alien!

Its head is pointed, not rounded like ours, with what looks like fur covering where we have hair. Its lower face is partially extended, like a snout but flatter and when it opens its mouth I see white teeth, but it has two fangs on the top set. Its nose is flat and square. It's shirtless but has on trousers of some kind. Its arms are longer than ours and skinny, ending in four long fingers. Its feet are bare as well and look more like a cats, with its legs slightly bowed in the middle. A long sharp looking tail curls around its leg, shaking with a rattle. But the weirdest thing is its skin colour. So different to any on Earth, a pale pink. Not like ours, but a bubblegum pink with dark pink lines running through it. It's beautiful, in an alien sort of way. It looks primal, and fierce and reminds me of my cat stalker. Pulling in my shock, I square my shoulders. I can freak out about seeing an alien later, I need to find my guys.

"Where are my friends?"

It tilts its head at me, its cat shaped eyes watching my every move. I don't let the fear in me rule me, I step forward with my hands outstretched.

"My friends?"

Of course, it does not speak English. Ugh, looking around, I point at the sleeping bags in the circle and then back to me. Its head swivels a few times as if trying to understand my meaning. I'm taking it as a good sign it hasn't attacked me yet. I repeat the actions again.

It nods and then opens its mouth, flashing fangs and sharp teeth. Grunts and strange noises, which I'm guessing is its language comes out of its mouth. Okay, Indy. Think. Watching it warily, I try to think of a plan. It steps towards me, its tail swaying as it walks. It moves more like an animal than a human, all grace and soft on its feet. I don't let myself step back or react, even when it towers over me. So close I can smell it, like earth after a rain. It smells like nature itself.

When I make no move, it's four-fingered hand lifts towards me. I stop myself from cringing, but all it does it pick up my hair curiously. It runs it through its fingers before it drops it. Its hand lifts again as it runs its fingers down my face as I talk.

"Look alien man, I need to find my friends so I can kick- HEY!"

I shout as it feels along my breasts. It jumps back and hisses, crouching down looking at me. Shit, okay.

"Bad alien. You didn't even buy me a drink first."

Its head cocks again, and I sigh. An idea pops into my head. I pound my chest lightly.

"Friend," I say, stretching out the letters. It tilts its head again before it's forked tongue slithers out, wetting its lips.

"Frrr..." It purrs the last, making me smile as it tries to copy me.

"Friend." I try again.

"Frenndd." The word ends on a growl from the handsy alien.

Okay, close enough. Nodding, I point from me to it then to the sleeping bags.

It follows my movements before looking back at me. It nods again.

"Frenndd." It steps back and starts walking away. It stops at the edge of the trees and gestures for me. Sighing at this insanity, I hurry after the alien, following it into the dark forest. When I find those guys, I'm going to kill them. I can't believe we have crashed on an alien planet and I'm following after an eight-foot house cat. With my new cat stalker at my side, I follow the alien into the strange forest in search of my four-sorta- boyfriends. It's been a hell of a year.

TRANSMISSION LOG 00310
DATE: 2032
MISSION: 43, COLONY
SHIP: DAWNBREAKER
DESTINATION: AYAMA

>.............. Accepted
> An attack on the ship damaged the hull,
resulting in complete computer and ship failure. Rebels killed guards and colonists alike
as they hacked the controls. Colony and crew
were evacuated to the emergency shuttles which
landed on the closest planet. The flight crew
stayed behind to offer them the best chance of
survival. The colonists and crew are scattered
across the unfamiliar world with no supplies
and no ship out of there. Send help, I repeat
Colony Mission 43 has crashed. Mayday. To
anyone that receives this, if you can track
this signal. Please save us.

ABOUT THE AUTHOR_

K.A. Knight is an indie author trying to get all of the stories and characters out of her head. She loves reading and devours every book she can get her hands on, she also has a worrying caffeine addiction.

She leads her double life in a sleepy English town, where she spends her days at the evil day job and comes home to her fur babies and wine.

Read more at K.A. Knight's website or join her Facebook Reader Group

Made in United States
Orlando, FL
01 February 2024

43176576R00105